"Let yourself go, Marisa. Don't fight."

Gabriel's voice was thick with desire as his body moved restlessly against her.

"I can't," Marisa moaned, shuddering. "I need time—don't rush me." She was at once fascinated and frightened, for Gabriel seemed out of control, his hands caressing her insistently, her body burning at his touch.

At her words he wrenched himself away from her, still tense with excitement. "You *have* changed, Marisa. At nineteen you were like an adolescent. Now you're more or less a woman."

"I'm not sure I like the way you phrased that!"

He gave her a mocking smile. "You won't be a woman until you stop running away from your feelings."

"I'm not running," she said, walking to the door. "I'm just thinking about it." Then she walked out.

CHARLOTTE LAMB
is also the author of these

Harlequin Presents

and these

Harlequin Romances

Many of these titles are available at your local bookseller.

For a free catalogue listing all available Harlequin Romances
and Harlequin Presents, send your name and address to:

HARLEQUIN READER SERVICE,
M.P.O. Box 707, Niagara Falls, NY 14302
Canadian address: Stratford, Ontario N5A 6W2

CHARLOTTE LAMB

abduction

Harlequin Books

TORONTO • LONDON • LOS ANGELES • AMSTERDAM
SYDNEY • HAMBURG • PARIS • STOCKHOLM • ATHENS • TOKYO

Harlequin Presents edition published June 1981
ISBN 0-373-10435-9

Original hardcover edition published in 1981
by Mills & Boon Limited

CHAPTER ONE

THE pavement was crowded with jostling shoppers loaded down with packages. Outside the library in the centre of the High Street, a group of children in scarves and woolly hats were singing Christmas carols by torchlight while one of them collected money from passers-by, shaking his collecting tin hopefully beneath their noses. The late afternoon sky had a threatening look. The temperature had dropped overnight and Marisa thought as she looked up at the dark sky that she would not be surprised if they were to have snow.

Jamie was tired and hungry. They were on their way home after a walk in the park. Marisa walked fast, her slender figure warmly wrapped in a sheepskin coat which still had an expensive look although it was now three years old. Most of her money went on clothes for Jamie. She hadn't been able to afford a new winter coat for herself.

Jamie suddenly pointed at a shop window, crowing and throwing himself about in his pushchair. Marisa stopped, smiling, so that he could admire the Christmas tree which had caught his eye.

'Pretty, isn't it?' she asked, bending to smile at him.

'Pitty,' Jamie said. He was beginning to talk,

5

but so far his vocabulary was small, and mangled, so that only Marisa was able to guess what he was saying.

Remembering that she had promised to bring Sally some cakes, Marisa hurried on to a shop two doors away and parked the pushchair.

'I won't be a minute, darling,' she promised Jamie, whose lower lip began to tremble. He gave her an accusing look.

'Bad.' It was one of his favourite words because it was one which even the dullest grown-up seemed to understand.

'I know,' she said, smiling. 'I'll be quick.' She hurried into the shop. Sally rarely asked her to do anything and it always made Marisa feel better to do something in return for all the kindness she and Jamie had had from her.

She was in such a rush that she ran full tilt into somebody, knocking all her parcels to the floor.

'Sorry,' she gasped, diving to pick them up.

The thin woman almost snatched her belongings away. No doubt she was tired and cross, like Jamie. Christmas was an exhausting season. Marisa apologised again, but only got a frosty glare.

'Oh, dear,' the baker said as she went up to the counter. 'Someone was in a nasty mood.'

Marisa smiled at him and ordered her cakes, watching him place them in a cardboard box which he then did up with string, tying a little loop so that Marisa could carry the box without trouble.

'Busy all day, I've been,' the baker said cheerfully. 'Good thing Christmas only comes once a year.'

'I love Christmas,' Marisa told him firmly, and he winked at her.

'That's the ticket!'

She handed him the money and waited for her change, looking at herself absently in the mirror behind him. Her face was flushed with the cold air, her blue eyes very bright. The long black hair which she normally wore tied back behind her head had escaped and was blowing around her face untidily. One of Jamie's favourite games was to undo her hair and tug at it, laughing.

'Thank you,' said the baker, giving her the change, and Marisa rushed out of the shop.

For a second she just looked blankly at the spot where she had left Jamie. Then she looked behind her in case she had put the pushchair on the other side of the shop doorway. It was only as her shocked mind took in the fact that the pushchair was nowhere to be seen that she felt her heart give a great, terrified lurch.

She ran to the corner and then back again in a rapid, confused search. All the colour had left her face and she was trembling. She had a dazed idea that she might have left Jamie outside the window which had attracted his attention earlier, so she ran back there and looked at the tinsel, the tall tree with its fairy and winking coloured lights.

'Oh, no,' she said to herself but aloud. 'Jamie!'

Her mind had not yet actually begun to think. She was just reacting, trying to convince herself that she had made a mistake, that this was not happening.

People were looking at her as they hurried past, recognising that she was behaving oddly. She looked around, still saying Jamie's name, as though expecting to see the pushchair and the cross, flushed, sulky little face.

A policeman was proceeding with calm, regulation pace towards her through the crowds. Marisa ran towards him, forgetting the cakes which fell from her hand and were trodden underfoot in a second by a startled lady in a red hat.

Clutching the uniformed arm, Marisa broke out in a trembling voice: 'My baby—someone has taken my baby!'

From under his helmet he surveyed her without panic. 'Where did you leave the baby, madam?'

'There,' said Marisa, pointing back towards the cake shop. 'Outside. I was buying cakes.'

'Are these yours?' The lady in the red hat handed her the squashed box with a half curious, half reproachful look. 'I'm sorry, I trod on them without seeing them.'

Marisa dazedly took them, still staring at the policeman. 'I was only in there for a minute, just one minute.'

'When was this, madam?'

'Just now.' Marisa's panic was growing. She felt like screaming to make him do something.

'They can't have gone far. I was only in there for a minute. I can't find him!' She looked away, trying to see something other than dense knots of hurrying people. There was a pushchair. Her heart leapt wildly until she saw the little girl in it. 'Please, do something!' she said to the policeman. 'Someone has taken him away. They can't have gone far.' It was the main thought in her mind. Whoever had taken Jamie must be wheeling him along the High Street if only she could see them—but in which direction? Where were they?

The policeman was talking into his walkie-talkie. He looked at her kindly, his smoothly shaven face calm. 'They're sending a car. It won't take long. We'll cruise around and maybe we'll spot the baby. Now don't worry, madam. Keep calm. We'll find your baby.'

The lady in the red hat had been joined by her husband. They were unashamedly listening, staring at Marisa.

'I suppose you didn't have someone with you?' asked the lady. 'You don't think a friend has just wheeled the baby on somewhere and will be back any minute?'

'No,' said Marisa.

'Was anyone with you, madam?' the policeman asked.

She shook her head. Her wide, terrified eyes kept searching the street. Her heart was racing inside her chest; her hands were so cold they were cramped. It was a nightmare, one she had

had years ago and from which she had fled, but here it was in reality. Maybe you could never run from anything.

'Have you got a friend who might have seen the pushchair and taken the baby a little way along the street?' the policeman asked.

'Who would do a thing like that?' Marisa muttered.

'People have got a funny sense of humour,' the policeman told her drily.

There were several other people standing beside them now, listening and watching in fascinated curiosity. A little crowd was forming. Marisa heard newcomers asking: 'What's up?' and heard people saying: 'Someone's taken her baby.'

Siren wailing, the police car was speeding down the High Street towards them. Other cars edged out of the way and the black vehicle screeched to a halt. The policeman went over and spoke to the man driving it, then beckoned to Marisa. She was bundled into the back of it and the driver turned and gave her a reassuring little smile.

'We'll drive first one way up the High Street, then turn and go back the other. You keep looking and if you spot the baby give us a shout.'

There was a woman police officer in the back beside her. She had a notebook in her hand and kept asking Marisa questions. While she stared desperately out of the window, her eyes hurting as she tried to see everything they passed, Marisa answered the questions.

'He was wearing a cream coat and had a brown woolly hat on. Yes, gloves, but he keeps taking them off. They're sewn into the arms of the coat.'

'Trousers?'

'Brown cord ones,' Marisa agreed.

'What about shoes?'

'Red ones. He takes them off too sometimes. And his socks.' Jamie had a passion for discarding his clothing. Sometimes when she went into a shop and left him outside she would come back to find shoes and socks littering the pavement.

The car had turned and was driving back slowly the other way. She stared and stared until her head ached, but there was no sign of Jamie.

'What am I going to do?' she kept saying. 'Where can he be?'

'What about your husband?' the woman police officer asked.

Marisa's face tightened. 'I haven't got one.'

The woman looked at her quickly. The driver glanced at her in the mirror above his head.

'You're not married?'

Marisa hesitated. She was staring out of the window. After a moment the woman asked again. 'You're not married, then?'

'We're separated,' Marisa said.

She felt the change in the atmosphere. 'Can I have your husband's name and address?' the woman asked.

'No,' said Marisa.

She was thinking hard. If she told them they would get in touch with him, and for two years Marisa had been running to escape him. She was not having him erupt into her life again.

'I'm afraid we'll have to have it,' the woman told her quite kindly.

Marisa shook her head, the long silky strands of hair brushing against her pale cheek. Strain was etching lines in her face, stripping the youth from it and tightening all the muscles. Her bloodless lips were trembling. The woman police officer watched her and then gave another look at her colleague, who shrugged his shoulders.

'Your husband could have taken the baby,' the woman said. 'Hasn't that occurred to you?'

Marisa half smiled, but the movement of her mouth was ironic and without real humour. 'No.'

'He might have done,' the woman urged. 'It often is the father in these cases, believe me. Especially if there's been trouble.'

'No,' Marisa repeated. Every time she saw a pushchair she felt her heart stop, her eyes staring until everything seemed to dissolve in front of her, but it was never Jamie. He had apparently vanished off the face of the earth.

'We only want to help you, my dear. We have to have your husband's name and address for our files, you see, and after all, he ought to be told. He is the baby's father.'

There was a silence. Then with another quick look, the woman asked: 'He is the father, I suppose?'

Marisa said bitterly, 'Oh, yes, but I don't want him told.' There was too much she could not say. The last thing in the world she wanted was for Gabriel to know where she was. Even in her dazed terror she held to that thought. They must not tell Gabriel.

The car stopped and she looked out. 'You stay in the car, my dear,' the policewoman said as she moved, her hand anchoring Marisa against the seat as she realised where they were.

The driver had got out and was walking up the path. Marisa watched him knock. Sally opened the door and stared at him, then looked past him at the car, her sensible round face puzzled. The policeman talked and Sally started forward, looking horrified. The policeman halted her, shaking his head.

'Just checking to see if the baby has been brought back,' the policewoman told Marisa. 'Is that a relative? Your mother?'

'My employer,' Marisa said dully. 'I work for her.'

'What do you do?'

'Sally runs an employment agency. I do secretarial work part time.'

The woman looked at the neat suburban semi-detached house. 'But you do live here?'

'I've got a flat over the garage.' If all this hadn't happened she would be there now, getting Jamie his tea while he played in his high chair and banged his rubber hammer demandingly.

Marisa could see Sally talking. The policeman

was writing things down in a notebook. What was he asking? What was Sally telling him? There wasn't much that Sally could tell. Marisa had not confided the truth to her. In some ways she had regretted having to hold back on Sally. Ever since the day she had walked into the employment agency and asked for a job, Sally had been kindness itself to her. She had been unbelievably lucky in meeting Sally that day. She hadn't realised she was pregnant until a month later and then she had been stricken with shock and alarm, but Sally had soothed her distress, puzzled by it but willing to do what she could.

'You ought to tell your husband, Marisa,' Sally had said gently, and Marisa had gone white and shaken her head. Whatever happened, Gabriel must not know.

Sally had tried to persuade her for a while, but when she realised that Marisa was quite fixed in her intention she had suggested that the problem of the future could be solved quite easily if Marisa went on working for her until she had the baby and then afterwards became a part-time secretary. It had been comparatively easy to arrange for Jamie to be looked after while Marisa was working. Marisa had hated leaving him with another woman, but she had had no choice. In order to keep them both she had worked in the mornings and Jamie had joined the family of a woman who lived nearby. There were several other small children for him to play with and he seemed to thrive on company. Marisa had been afraid he would suffer in some way, but things had worked out very well.

The policeman came back down the path. Sally was with him. She looked at Marisa through the window. 'Are you all right?'

Marisa nodded, shivering.

'I'm sure they'll find him.' Sally clearly did not know what to say. She was almost as distressed as Marisa. Sally was nearly sixty, a woman with a fresh complexion and faded blue eyes. Her husband, Joe, was an invalid who had to be lifted in and out of his wheelchair but who had a slow, infectious sense of humour despite his bodily weakness. He had had a stroke several years ago, and Sally had taken over the running of the firm and was making a good job of it. Every day a neighbour took over the care of the house and Joe for a few hours while Sally went off to the agency. At first Marisa had been afraid that she was merely adding to Sally's problems, but Sally had told her with a smile that she had made life much easier.

Sally adored Jamie. She had no children of her own and her husband's stroke had frightened her, bringing her face to face with the possibility of a lonely, empty future. The advent of Jamie into their lives had given them a new lease of life. Both Sally and Joe loved to look after him for an hour or so, almost pleading with Marisa to go out so that they could have Jamie with them for a short time.

Sally looked at her hands and Marisa realised

she was still clutching the battered box of cakes.
She offered them to Sally. 'Sorry, they got trodden on.'

'Oh, my dear!' Sally exclaimed, tears coming
into her eyes. She brushed them away and looked
at the policewoman. 'Can't I come with her?'

'It would be best if you stayed here,' the
woman said. 'In case someone brings him back.'

'She should have someone with her,' Sally said.

'We'll look after her.'

Marisa wanted Sally to come, but there was
Joe. He couldn't be left alone. And someone
might bring Jamie home. It might have been a
mistake. She had an awful feeling that she had
left Jamie somewhere else, that he was sitting in
his pushchair waiting for her somewhere. The
events of the last hour had blurred in her mind.
There was an unreality about the whole thing
which left her dazed. She couldn't believe all this
was happening. It had to be a mistake, a nightmare, she thought. The nightmare she had once
run from but which had caught up with her.

'If you need me, love,' said Sally, reaching
through the open window to touch her arm tentatively.

'Yes, thank you.' Marisa saw the tears in
Sally's eyes and wished she could cry. She
wanted to, but the tears merely stung and blinded
her behind her eyes. They did not escape or relieve this awful fear.

The car sped away and the policewoman said:
'We'll find him, don't worry. Probably some

lonely woman borrowed him, but we'll get him back. He'll be okay. I expect he's being well looked after—spoilt, probably. That's what usually happens. Someone who's lost a baby gets a bit desperate and does something foolish. But she'll be making a big fuss of little Jamie, you'll see. Your friend was right, though—you shouldn't be alone. A bit of a strain, isn't it? You need someone with you. Be sensible, love, give us your husband's name and address and we'll get in touch with him and whatever you've quarrelled about, he'll come round, you mark my words. He'll be as worried as you are. After all, it is his baby too.'

Marisa didn't answer. She stared out of the window at the brightly lit shops with their Christmas displays. The streets were still packed with people, forcing their way along the busy pavements, their faces flushed and worried.

'You'll have to tell us sooner or later,' the policewoman said in a sharper voice.

The car slid round to the modern police station and parked. The policewoman touched Marisa's arm. 'Out you get, love.'

Marisa got out. Her legs weren't very steady. She stumbled and the other woman supported her, looking into her white face.

'What you need is a cup of tea. I could do with one myself.'

The car drove off and Marisa let the woman guide her into the police station. A sergeant behind the desk stared at her and after a murmur

of consultation Marisa was steered through the
reception area into a small waiting room. She sat
down obediently without a word and the policewoman sat down, too. 'They'll bring us some tea in
a minute,' she promised. 'I just want to go over
what you've told me. I might have missed a few
things.'

'I feel sick,' Marisa said, swallowing. She half
rose and the woman quickly showed her into a
small white-tiled lavatory. Marisa swayed, her
forehead dewed with chilly perspiration. Her
whole body was icy. Sickness came and went in
waves.

She heard the policewoman talking in the
further room and after washing her face with cold
water she went back. There was tea standing on
the unpolished desk. Marisa sat down and
accepted one of the mugs. The warmth of the hot
liquid reached her as she took the mug between
both hands, and she sipped, leaning over the
desk, shuddering.

'I'm scared,' she whispered, almost to herself.
'He's so little.' Jamie was all she had in the
world. She could not even begin to imagine a life
without him. It seemed impossible that only two
years ago Jamie had not existed. He had woven
himself into her life, her heart, and she was sick
with terror as she tried to make herself think
about what might have happened to him.

'We're looking for him,' the policewoman as-
sured her. 'Don't think about anything except
how you're going to help us find him. I don't

want to press you, but we've got to have the father's name.'

Marisa drank some more of the tea. It scalded her throat, but it did something to lessen the iciness of her skin.

'How old are you, my dear?' The policewoman was trying another track now.

'Twenty-three,' Marisa answered. She felt much older. She felt about a hundred. Her skin seemed to be too tight for her bones. They ached as they pressed against it, her white face all angles and sharp lines.

'Where did you live before you came here?'

'I'm a Londoner,' Marisa said. 'I've always lived here.'

'Which part?'

'All over London.' Marisa had been an only child. Her parents had been restless, impulsive people who had moved all the time. She had never lived anywhere for long, constantly moving to new areas, new schools, finding new friends but always losing the old ones. She had hated the perpetual change which made up her life. She had longed for permanence and a settled home, and she had never had it.

The policewoman stared at her accusingly. She was a young woman of Marisa's age, sturdily built and sensible, with a high colour and sharp not unkindly brown eyes.

'You do want to help us find your baby, don't you?'

'Of course I do,' Marisa said in a high, shaking

voice. 'But what help is it to you to know where I lived before I came here?'

'It might help us to know anything about you,' the woman explained. 'The baby might have been taken by someone who knows you, someone from your past life.' She paused. 'Your husband.'

'No,' Marisa said.

The woman leaned back in her chair and played with her pencil, tapping it on the desk. 'We could be here quite a while,' she said. 'Do you mind if I call you Marisa? That's a pretty name—unusual. Was it the one you got when you were a baby or did you make it up yourself?' She smiled as she asked that, becoming very friendly, trying to put Marisa at her ease and slacken the tension in the little room.

'It's my own name. My mother chose it.'

'You said your mother was dead, earlier?'

'Yes. She and my father are both dead.'

'Where did they live? Around here?'

'Blackheath.' She stared into the empty mug. For the last three years of their life they had settled at Blackheath, but she had always had the feeling that they might sell their house and move again any moment. They liked the Heath. They had a dog by then, the first pet they had ever owned, and they took it for walks across the Heath twice a day. Marisa had no longer lived with them; she had had a bedsitting-room in Camden Town. She visited them from time to time, but her parents had somehow never been close to her. They were too involved with them-

selves. A child had always been too much of a tie
to them, an extra piece of luggage for them to
carry around. She often thought they found it
hard to remember who she was.

The policewoman watched her, trying to judge
what she was thinking from her expression.

The room was very quiet, very impersonal,
very clean. It smelt of floor polish and dust.
Marisa was having trouble believing in anything. As a child she had often felt unreal. The
upheavals and changes had left her with a sense
of being alienated, alone. Jamie had made her feel
involved in life—but now Jamie was not there
and unreality was wrapping her round and stifl-
ing her.

'You don't smoke?' The policewoman's voice
made her jump.

'No.' She shook her head.

'More tea?'

'No, thank you.' She looked at the clock on the
wall. It kept up a steady, rhythmical beat. How
long was it since Jamie vanished? She tried to
remember, but time had lost all significance.

The questions began again, and she answered
them absently, hardly knowing what she was
saying by now. The tick-tick of the clock became
a sound her blood picked up rather than her ears.
When the other woman was silent Marisa just
stared at the clock.

There was a pattern to the questions, she felt,
but she didn't know what it was, she couldn't
grasp it. The woman was not unkind, but her

eyes were watchful. Marisa felt that there was no warmth coming out of her. She almost felt she was being suspected of something, but what?

Restlessly she looked at the clock again. 'Can't you ask if there's any news? It's hours since . . .'

'If there was any news someone would come and tell us. Where was Jamie born? In hospital? That would be St Mary's, would it?'

'Yes.' It was a vast, anonymous hospital set in tidily kept gardens which were mostly lawn. The nurses bustled to and fro in the wards without ever seeming to care much about their patients. The wards were too big and too busy. Patients were moved in and out of them like robots. There was never time for a nurse to get to know a patient. Marisa had had the baby and been sent home within a week because her bed was needed. London was badly in need of more hospitals and those which existed were understaffed and over-worked.

'Who's your doctor?'

'Dr. Sullivan.' Marisa had only seen him about half a dozen times. He was busy, too. He had far too many patients and far too little time. When she did go to see him he scarcely looked at her, writing out a prescription almost before she had finished speaking, passing it to her with a brief glance before banging on his bell as she found her way out.

'What does your husband do?'

Marisa wouldn't have known how to answer that even if she had wanted to. What did Gabriel do? He had never discussed it with her and she had never asked. Their marriage had been so short and had had the same air of unreality that she was feeling now. When she thought about those months she felt they had happened to someone else, except that Jamie was too solid a consequence for them to have been imaginary.

Gabriel was real, all right. He existed somewhere outside her world. Circling like a dark satellite over her head, his orbit was too far from her own for him to find her.

She put a trembling hand up to her hair and brushed it back from her face. Her fingertips felt icy. They looked shrunken, the way they did if she stayed in the bath too long. Pruny fingers, she used to tease Jamie as she fished him out of his bath. He had his bath before he went to bed. He wouldn't get into it unless his yellow submarine was at hand so that he could play with it while she soaped him, the plump wriggling little body like an eel between her hands.

The door opened and a tall quiet man came into the room. Marisa looked at him sharply, hopefully, with fear.

'Is there any news?'

He gave her a calming smile and said: 'Not yet. Don't worry, Mrs Radley.'

The policewoman got up and went over to the door. The two of them had a whispered conversation. Marisa stared at them and then looked at the clock. Hours. She had been here for hours. The time went drivingly on and nothing happened except questions, more and more questions. Were they looking for Jamie? What were they doing?

'She's a funny one,' the policewoman said in a very low voice.

'What do you think?' the man asked.

'Can't make up my mind,' the woman answered, then they both turned and looked at Marisa.

The man wandered over and the woman went out for a moment, only to come back and resume her seat. The man offered Marisa a cigarette and when she refused asked if she would mind if he smoked. She shook her head.

'Are they looking for him? Someone must have seen him. I was only in the shop for a minute.'

The man drew on his cigarette, watching her. He had impassive thoughtful eyes. She hadn't got a clue what he was thinking.

'I'm afraid we're going to have to insist that you give us your husband's name and address, Mrs Radley. It's essential. If you really want us to find your son we're going to need your co-operation.'

A tremor ran through her. She averted her face and didn't answer. The man smoked, watching her. He glanced at the other woman and gave a shrugging gesture. 'Let's see your notebook.'

The woman handed it to him. He flicked over the pages, frowning over the writing. 'I can't read half of this. I suppose you know what it says.' His voice had a wry irritation.

'It's like trying to get blood out of a stone,' the woman sighed. 'Obstinate isn't the word.'

The man handed her back the notebook and looked at Marisa. 'I suppose you did really have Jamie with you?'

She looked at him, startled, her blue eyes enormous. For a second she thought seriously about it. Had she made a mistake? Was Jamie at home? Then she remembered the park, the swings, the Christmas tree in the shop window. No.

'He was with me,' she said. 'I left him outside while I got the cakes. He was cross.'

'He was cross, was he?' The man smiled at her gently. 'Were you cross, Mrs Radley? Tired, maybe? You didn't get angry with Jamie, did you? Sometimes mothers can get so tired they do things they would never do if they were feeling themselves. Don't be afraid to tell us. We understand how these things happen.'

She looked at him in bewilderment. 'What things? What are you talking about?'

'Maybe you hit Jamie a bit harder than you intended to,' he said softly. 'You're very young yourself. I've got a daughter your age and she has a little boy. Young mothers can get very tense.'

She flushed suddenly, her eyes angry. 'I've never hit Jamie! I wouldn't hit him. He's all I have in the world.' The suggestion sent a fierce shock of pain through her. She hadn't understood until that moment, but now she saw what they suspected and she was horrified. She looked at the policewoman accusingly. 'Is that what you think? That I've done something to Jamie, that I'm lying? I'm not! I'm not lying. Someone has taken him. He was with me and I left him outside that shop and when I got out someone had taken him.' She was so angry that the words rushed out of her red hot, tumbling over each other. 'Are you looking for him? While you've been asking me all these questions, have you been looking for my baby?'

The man straightened and flicked his cigarette to the floor, treading on it. 'We're looking, Mrs Radley,' he said, and went out.

The policewoman was less watchful, her manner slightly easier. 'We have to be sure,' she said. 'These things do happen. Don't worry, everything is being done. Everyone who was in the vicinity is being asked to come forward with any information about you or Jamie. We've got loudspeaker vans touring the area of the High Street. There've been dozens of phone calls already.'

'Someone must have seen Jamie,' Marisa said. Would anyone remember a little boy with brown curls and a pink, cross face? All those crowds, the great anonymous mass of faces, surely someone must have seen Jamie and must remember?

'You ought to eat,' the policewoman told her. 'I'm starving, myself. You've been here hours. You must be hungry.'

Marisa shook her head. She couldn't have eaten to save her life. Her stomach was churning. She would be sick again if she even smelt food.

'Have another cup of tea, at least,' she was urged, and accepted reluctantly.

'Would you like to lie down for a while?' The

policewoman watched her drinking the tea, noting the pallor, the telltale dark stains beneath her eyes.

Marisa couldn't have rested. She was too on edge, her nerves flickering constantly as though she were in deadly danger.

'You're on the radio,' she was told. 'They're broadcasting an appeal to anyone who saw you or Jamie to come forward.'

Suddenly Marisa's whole body jerked. She sat up, looking at the woman in distraught shock. 'Broadcast? My name?' That hadn't occurred to her until now. Her name broadcast, sent out across London on the radio?

Puzzled, the policewoman said: 'The evening papers have got the story too. They managed to pick up a snapshot of you from the lady whose house you live in . . .'

Marisa swayed, her head falling forward to rest on the table. The policewoman ran forward to her. 'Are you all right? What's wrong?'

Marisa was swimming in misty seas, her mind submerged beneath waves of ice-cold shock. She wasn't even conscious of the other woman's presence. Her body was limp, her skin damp with perspiration.

'You should lie down, my dear,' the policewoman told her, bending over her. 'Would you like me to get a doctor? Are you faint?'

Marisa struggled to pull herself back from the darkness that was threatening to engulf her. She had to think, to work out what to do. She couldn't just let go, tempting though the thought was, because she had to work things out.

She forced herself upright, her slender body shivering, the fine bones of her pale face visible beneath the taut skin.

'I'm all right,' she whispered.

The door behind them was suddenly flung open and the policewoman glanced round. An angry voice was raised. 'You can't go in there!'

A man filled the doorway, his black head almost touching the top of the frame. He was wearing an expensively tailored dark overcoat which hung open. A white silk evening scarf blew across his dark evening suit as he strode forward. His face was harsh and powerful; the close-shaven jaw assertive, the mouth straight and very hard. The policewoman took in the details of his appearance with surprise, but he wasn't even looking at her. He was staring with fixed eyes at Marisa, who was still drooping slightly in the chair.

She looked round, half afraid of what she might see, as if she had suddenly felt the new presence in the room even in her dazed condition.

Her white lips parted. 'No!' she whispered.

Then she fell sideways from the chair in a dead faint.

CHAPTER TWO

MARISA felt as though there were lead weights on her eyelids. She struggled to force her eyes open, wincing at the beating pain inside her head. She couldn't remember where she was, finding the stark unshaded light of the little room intrusive as it flashed on her sight. She was lying on a hard bed. The wall facing her was painted cream, a dull flat colour that was oddly depressing.

She turned her head slowly and met watchful grey eyes. At once her mind jerked awake and she remembered.

'Oh, God,' she muttered, looking away.

'Lie still.' He sounded curt. The terrible familiarity of that deep, harsh tone sank into her. It was a sensation she was far too intimate with— this helpless, bitter weakness.

For a moment she lay there, trembling, accepting that her flight was over. Gabriel had found her. She had known he would from the moment she realised her photograph had been put into the newspaper. She hadn't expected his arrival to be so soon. Or had time blurred to such an extent that she no longer knew what time it was? How long had she been here? How long had Jamie been missing?

'Jamie,' she said hoarsely, turning back to him again. Her blue eyes were strained and over-bright with unshed tears. 'Is there any news? Have they found him?'

'Not yet,' he said, his mouth straight. 'But they will, don't worry.'

'Don't worry? How can you say don't worry? I'm going out of my mind!'

'I realise that, but you've got to believe they'll find him. You mustn't let yourself think otherwise.'

'Mustn't I?' She laughed without humour, her mouth trembling. 'What would you know about it? Oh, *you* would think you could just order me not to worry, not to think anything forbidden. Your mind is so convenient. You flick a switch and it does what you tell it, does it? You're not a human being. You're a machine, a computer, programmed to print out what's wanted, not to have any ideas it hasn't been programmed with, ordinary little human thoughts like love or fear or panic.'

'You're hysterical,' he said, his dark brows a heavy line across his forehead. 'They're getting a doctor—God knows why they didn't get one before. What have they been doing to you? Have they kept you in that room pestering you with questions in this state?'

'Why did you have to come?' Marisa turned away, sighing so deeply her slender body was wrenched with it. 'Why didn't you stay away? I can put up with the police questions, but I can't put up with you.'

'That's too bad,' he muttered grimly. 'I'm your husband. I have a right to be with you.'

'Rights! That's all you understand!'

'I understand a lot more than that,' Gabriel told her, his eyes on her disturbed face. 'I understand that I have a son I've never even seen and didn't know existed.'

Marisa drew in a shaken breath and didn't answer. Her blue eyes flickered restlessly, not touching his powerful figure, moving around the room like something in search of a safe hiding place.

'How dared you give birth to my child and not tell me?' he asked curtly. 'Hadn't I the right to know I had a son?'

She closed her mouth, not answering, not looking at him. Her body tensed on the bed, drawing in on itself, trying to stop the trembling in her limbs.

'I gather he's eighteen months old. You must have been aware that you were pregnant when you ran out on me.'

Marisa didn't say a word. She was trying hard not to listen to what he was saying. She didn't want to talk to him.

'Is he mine?' His voice grew savage, a raw feeling in it.

Her head swung on a reflex impulse. 'Yes!'

Gabriel's taut body relaxed and she suddenly wished she had not answered, wished she had lied to him. She had spoken without thinking, but now she saw that it might have been better to tell him Jamie was not his child. Why hadn't she thought of that?

Gabriel leaned towards her, his sinewy hands

tightening on the back of the chair he sat on. 'What does he look like?' His voice was husky and the grey eyes had a brilliance which betrayed emotion.

Her blue eyes closed and she gave a shuddering groan. 'Don't!' She couldn't talk about Jamie with this fear pressing on her heart. She could list the details of his hair colour, his eyes, his clothes—but that wouldn't tell Gabriel the things that really mattered about Jamie. It wouldn't show him what Jamie was really like. The details that would do that were too painful to talk about. What could she say? He likes his eggs boiled lightly and doesn't like the taste of spinach? He sleeps on his face with his bottom stuck up in the air? He chews everything you give him. His teddy bear is half digested already and he pulls all the buttons off his clothes. When he tries to walk he often falls over, but he always gets up again and tries not to cry. He gets earache when the weather is cold and dogs frighten him although he won't show it.

She could, of course, say, he's a lot like you. He's going to be tall. His body is long and muscular. He has big hands and feet, for a baby, and his hair flops over his eyes just the way yours does when you bend your head. Jamie had brown hair, not black, but he had the strong bones of his father, the assertive, masculine pugnacity of the jawline. When he was in a temper his eyes could flash and his mouth could go straight and brooding. How many times had she seen Gabriel in him and been close to tears?

But she wouldn't say any of that to him. She kept her eyes shut and wished he would go away, because the pain of having him in the same room was killing her.

The door opened and the policewoman came in followed by a short man in a brown suede coat, who looked tired. 'The doctor, sir,' the policewoman said with a courtesy that told Marisa that she now knew who Gabriel was and that the usual kaleidoscopic change had come over everything. Until now the police had been treating Marisa with calmly polite suspicion, but as she looked round the policewoman gave her a nervous, curious smile.

No doubt she was devoured with curiosity. Gabriel didn't need to explain himself to anyone. He stood up, dwarfing the doctor, his broad shoulders tense.

'Can you give her something to calm her down? She's hysterical. She should have been given some treatment long ago. They've been grilling her like some murder suspect when she's obviously in a state of traumatic shock.'

'I don't want anything,' said Marisa, sitting up, her ruffled black hair flung against her shoulder.

The doctor took off his coat and gave her a little smile, taking her wrist between finger and thumb. 'All a bit of a strain, isn't it? Have you taken anything? No pills?'

She shook her head. 'I don't want to be sedated. I won't take any pills.' She wanted to know what was happening. If they gave her a sedative she would float in a grey, amorphous

cloud and not be sure what was going on around
her, and she had to stay clear-headed as far as she
could.

'How do you feel? A bit tired, hmm?' He
pulled up one of her eyelids, shone a light into
her eyes. 'Look up, would you? Sideways?'

Marisa obeyed, a flare of irritation making her
blue eyes flash. 'I'm perfectly all right,' she insisted.

'You'll feel terrible if you don't get some
sleep,' the doctor told her blandly. He smiled at
her, a professional, impersonal smile which had
watchful sharpness behind it. 'Must sleep, you
know. I realise it sounds callous, but your body
isn't a machine, you can't run it without switch-
ing off now and then or you'll blow a fuse.'

'I don't want a sedative!'

'Something to calm you down, make it easier to
cope,' he said, walking over to where he had put
down his large black case. Marisa saw him bend
over it, watched him turn round again, a hypo-
dermic in his hand, and said angrily: 'I'm not a
child! I don't have to accept that, and I refuse to
be sedated.'

Gabriel had not moved, his tall body looming
beside her in silence, his hands thrust into his
pockets. Now he said: 'Can she be moved? Can
she leave here? She isn't under suspicion of
having done anything. In these surroundings she
won't get any rest.'

The doctor glanced at the policewoman. She
shrugged. Gabriel bit out: 'Do I have to get my
solicitor to deal with it?'

The policewoman withdrew without a word. Gabriel looked at Marisa restlessly. 'Let the doctor give you something to steady your nerves.'

'My nerves are fine.'

'Don't be so damned obstinate!'

'I think it's your nerves that need calming,' Marisa muttered. 'But then they always have.'

The doctor looked down discreetly, moving back as though moving out of the line of fire. Gabriel eyed Marisa grimly, his dark face shuttered. She could see his temper rising. When Gabriel was angry his mouth became a hard, fierce line and his grey eyes burnt with inner rage. The doctor's face was familiar, too. How often had she seen people reacting like that when Gabriel was angry? He went around the world surrounded by people eager to soothe and placate him, jumping when he barked, running to do his bidding like nervous dogs.

'We'll get you out of here,' he said now, brusquely. 'We'll get you home and into bed.'

'That would be an excellent idea,' the doctor agreed, raising his head.

Marisa laughed in hollow irony. 'If by home you mean your house, forget it. I don't live there.'

'Damn you!' Gabriel broke out, that flash of his eyes making her spine stiffen.

The doctor turned round and began to fiddle with his case, putting on his coat again, as if to make it clear he wasn't listening.

'You don't want to stay here,' Gabriel pointed out, looking around the dull little room.

'I'll go back to my own flat.' It would be full of Jamie. His toys would be lined up on the shelf in his tiny bedroom. His cot would be empty. His high chair would be. standing in front of the window. But there would be no Jamie. Her heart winced convulsively. How was she going to bear it?

'You can't,' said Gabriel in a harsh voice. 'The press are crawling about all over the place like ants. They'd eat you alive.'

She was shocked into silence. Their eyes met. 'They know?' she managed to ask drily.

'What do you think?' His mouth twisted. Cynicism darkened his features. 'There was a reporter standing around in the police station when I walked in—he heard me talking to the desk sergeant. I practically had to knock him down to get away from him. I've no doubt the station is knee-deep in them by now.'

The doctor turned, his case in his hand. 'I'm afraid that's true, Mrs Radley.'

Marisa put her hands over her face. She couldn't go back to the quiet little flat over the garage. Sally and Joe must be wondering what had hit them. She wished vainly she could see them, explain, apologise.

'There's only one place where you'll be safe,' Gabriel told her.

'Safe?' Marisa flung the word back, lowering her hands.

Gabriel flushed angrily, his hard face tautening. 'Yes,' he said in a deep, thick voice. 'Quite safe.'

'From the press,' Marisa retorted, her blue eyes mocking and bitter.

His colour deepened. 'Yes.' His eyes slid sideways to encompass the doctor who was listening. 'The problem is—how are we going to get her out of here without running the gauntlet of the press?'

'The way I came in,' the doctor suggested. 'The police car park is at the back here. The press can't get in there—there are great iron gates to keep them out. You can go out the back and drive straight out past the reporters without them being able to get near you.'

'I'd rather stay here,' Marisa said desperately. 'In case . . .'

'There's nothing you can do. If there's any news it will come to you right away. You'll be kept fully informed, don't worry.' Gabriel looked at her with impatience, his face angular. 'I've offered a reward for information.'

She drew in her lower lip, her face wry with pain and brittle cynicism. 'Money,' she said. 'Of course, that's all you know, isn't it? Your only answer to anything.'

'It may help!' Gabriel stared back at her, his jaw pugnacious. 'If money will help, why shouldn't I try it? He's my son, even if you wish he wasn't.'

'Wish he wasn't? I'd give the earth to know he wasn't,' Marisa said hoarsely.

The dark colour flowed out of Gabriel's hard face. His bones tightened and his mouth clamped into a bitter line. 'Thank you.'

In the weeks before she left him there had been scenes like this, vicious scenes like a running battle, with each of them delivering ruthless blows which left scars. She had found it too painful to bear any longer. She had run and kept on running ever since. During the two years since they had seen each other nothing had changed. The bitter feeling between them still raged like a forest fire, burning everything in its path, leaving blackened earth behind it.

She swung her legs off the bed and swayed as she stood up. Gabriel moved to put an arm round her, but she pushed him away. 'I can manage.'

He moved back slightly, his powerful body tense with suppressed emotion. 'I'll have to send out a message,' he told the doctor. 'My chauffeur is waiting outside.'

'I'm just on my way,' the doctor answered, walking to the door. 'I'll give it to him. What do you want me to say?'

Gabriel bit his lower lip. 'I'll write a note.' He fished inside his pockets vaguely, frowning. The doctor sighed and opened his case again, produced a small white pad.

'How about this?'

'Thank you.' Gabriel ripped off a sheet and scribbled hurriedly, tucked the note into a brown envelope which the doctor gave him. Offering the man the note, he said drily: 'It's a black Rolls.'

The doctor half smiled and went out. Marisa was supporting herself with one hand on the back of a chair. Pulses were beating at her wrist and throat. She was finding it hard to concentrate on anything but thoughts of Jamie. If only she hadn't stopped outside that shop! If only she was back in the quiet little flat with Jamie in his cot asleep, his pink face buried in the mattress and the bedclothes humped over his bottom. It had worried her at first when he was a small baby.

'Should he sleep on his face? Won't he suffocate?' she had asked the baby clinic, and the nurse had smiled and shaken her head.

'Let him sleep the way he wants to sleep.'

Old ladies often stopped the pram to warn her that it was dangerous and Marisa had got used to explaining that it was quite safe. They never believed her, of course, and went away looking worried. She had found that a baby was a passport. People were always stopping to look into the pram, cooing over Jamie, waving his rattle at him while he stared back bolt-eyed. Older women often underestimated Marisa's age, especially when she was in jeans and a cotton T-shirt, and tried to give her motherly advice on how to look after him. She had made many friends in the busy district because Jamie gave people an excuse for talking to her. People needed an excuse. You couldn't just walk up to a stranger and get into conversation, but a baby was universally recognised as an accepted talking point, among women, at least.

Marisa had built her whole world around the fact of Jamie. Her day was governed by him. Her thoughts were absorbed by him.

Now she was left panic-stricken at the idea that she might never see him again.

Every time her thoughts approached that point she sheered away, her body jerking in pain.

She wouldn't think like that. The police would find Jamie and he would be safe and well. Who had taken him? Who would do such a wicked thing? The policewoman had said it might be some desperate, lonely woman in need of a child to love, and Marisa prayed that that was what had happened. So long as Jamie was being looked after and loved somewhere, he was safe. And the police would find him sooner or later. The alternative was too bitter to consider.

'I've told Harris to drive to the tube station half a mile away,' said Gabriel, looking at her. 'We'll get the police to drive us there to meet him.'

Marisa made no comment. Gabriel opened the door and she heard him talking to someone, his voice authoritative.

'Ready?' he asked, turning towards her. Behind him she saw a man in police uniform.

Marisa walked out of the room, feeling half dead. They went out along a narrow gloomy corridor and through a door into the police car park. A car waited, blue light flashing on top of it. Gabriel slid Marisa into the back and joined her. The door slammed and the car shot forward. Marisa felt Gabriel grasp her and push her down with her head below the level of the window. For a second she didn't understand, then she realised and gave a grim little smile.

There was a confused sound of shouting voices and the car accelerated, speeding away. Marisa was released and tremblingly sat up.

'They're following us,' said the police driver, watching the road behind him in the mirror. 'Want me to lose them?'

'Yes,' Gabriel commanded.

'Right,' the driver said, a peculiar satisfaction in his tone. He was grinning as though it was all a game.

The car roared and spun round a corner, raced down the little road, almost terrifying a man with a dog who was about to step out of his gate, then spun round another corner at top speed. Marisa closed her eyes and clung to the seat with both hands. She hated fast cars. She hated speed.

Gabriel put an arm round her. She stiffened and sat upright, pushing his hand down, and his arm fell away.

The car was almost at the tube station. Marisa saw the black Rolls waiting. The driver got out, dropped his cigarette and trod on it, opened the back door of the sleek car.

The police car screeched to a halt. Gabriel leapt out and helped Marisa carefully on to the pavement. Her legs weren't very steady. She stumbled and he half carried her to the Rolls and put her into it. A moment later the car was streaking away.

Marisa lay back against the seat, trembling, her eyes closed. Gabriel shifted beside her and leaned forward. She heard him talking on the phone hooked beneath his seat.

She didn't bother to listen. Waves of icy misery were flooding over her. She wanted to talk to someone, but not to Gabriel. To Sally, perhaps. Sally knew Jamie. They could have talked about him. She felt oddly as though she had imagined Jamie, as though he had been a dream. She needed to talk to someone who loved him the way she loved him, remembered him the way she remembered him. Pulling herself up with a start of fear, she realised she was thinking as though Jamie no longer existed. She must not think like that, she told herself. That was madness.

Jamie was the first human being she had ever felt secure with, he was the anchor which had held her firmly in life. Ever since he entered her life she had felt alive, real, secure. There had been nights when she first brought him home from the hospital when she had hung over his cot listening to him breathing anxiously because she was so scared he might stop. It had been such soft, gentle breathing, a mere whisper of sound. It had taken her weeks to accept that Jamie was strong, he was alive, he was not going to stop breathing if she did not watch over his cot.

Gabriel replaced the phone and shifted to face her, his long legs stretched out across the carpeted floor of the car.

'We'll be home in five minutes.'

Home, she thought. Why does he keep using that word? That damned great house isn't home to me, it never was, it was just the place where he kept me, the enormous doll's house for his new doll.

There was a little group of men outside the gates as they drove up. Gabriel leaned back, secure in the knowledge that both he and Marisa were only half visible behind their smoked glass windows. The tall iron gates were swung open and the car shot through. The gates clanged behind them, although some of the reporters tried to get through after the car.

Marisa looked up at the classical Palladian façade. It was immaculately maintained. It probably looked even better than when it was first built. Gabriel lavished money on it. He did most of his entertaining here when he was in London. It made a good showcase, impressing foreign businessmen and discreetly underlining Gabriel's wealth.

She could remember with appalling clarity the day she first saw it. She had felt very small and very young as Gabriel drove her through those gates and her wide, scared eyes looked up at the house. She had felt like running away. She had known at once that she was never going to feel she belonged in there.

She had been twenty years old, but she had felt about ten as Gabriel guided her out of the car and led her towards the smoothly stuccoed portico.

It had been impossible for her to explain to Gabriel how she felt. At that stage she had scarcely dared to say a single word to him. She could only stare at him from under her lashes, dazed and incredulous, not really believing that she was genuinely his wife.

How could Gabriel understand how she felt?

To him it was all routine, something he knew and found quietly familiar. He took for granted his sleek cars, his elegant expensive clothes, his beautiful houses and the discreet servants who ran them for him and attended to his every need. He might realise that it was all strange and disturbing for Marisa, but there was too great a gulf fixed between them for Gabriel to make the imaginative leap necessary to understand the depth of her shock.

They had only known each other for a few weeks, then. Marisa hadn't a clue how to talk to him. She hadn't a clue what made him tick. She did not know why he had married her or what he thought about, felt.

She knew why she had married him. It was something she preferred not to think about, but she knew the reason and shrank away from it.

Gabriel helped her out of the car and steered her rapidly towards the house. Behind them the reporters bayed at the gates, their cameras flashing. All they would get were back views of them hurrying inside the front door, but they were determined to get something.

The door closed behind them. Marisa felt it as though it were the clang of prison bars.

She was back in this house from which she had fled two years ago. She stood there, looking round the spacious hall. It had not changed an inch.

The bland cream and gold gleamed under an enormous chandelier. Gilt medallions decorated the smooth walls. A white porcelain shell held a fan of pink carnations which were reflected in a gilt framed mirror behind them.

The bald-headed man in a dark suit facing them was familiar, too. He was looking at Marisa hesitantly, his expressionless eyes probing her white face.

Gabriel did not give him a chance to speak. He took Marisa's elbow and urged her towards the stairs. 'You must lie down,' he said. 'You're exhausted.' Over his shoulder he said crisply to the butler: 'Have some supper sent up to Mrs Radley's bedroom at once. Something light.'

Marisa almost felt she floated up the wide staircase. She had had dreams of doing that, strange menacing dreams when her body felt light and unreal and the elegant hall looked nightmarish under that glittering chandelier.

The bedroom was just as she had left it. Everything was in its place, carefully dusted and preserved, each object painfully familiar to her as she looked around.

Gabriel had had it decorated for her after their marriage. His room was next door. The communicating door stood open, and she looked at it with a sharp pang of alarm.

Gabriel walked over and closed it and turned the lock, taking out the key. He came back and handed it to her.

A sudden flush stained her cheeks. She took the key, her face averted.

'I'm not totally insensitive,' he said in a harsh voice.

Marisa looked down at the deep white carpet, her toe tracing a pattern on it. The cold metal of the key warmed in her palm.

Gabriel walked over to the delicate white and gold French dressing-table and opened a drawer. He took out a filmy nightdress and tossed it on to the bed.

'Get undressed and into bed,' he said without looking at her.

Marisa did not move, her head still bent, an obstinate expression on her face.

Gabriel moved to the door and opened it again. 'I'll come back in five minutes,' he said, going out.

Marisa stood there for a moment, shivering. Slowly she went over to the bed and picked up the nightdress. Gabriel had taken the first one he found. He probably didn't remember seeing her in it, but Marisa remembered. She held the soft drift of lemon material in her hands, staring down at it. She had worn it on the last night Gabriel slept with her.

She closed her eyes, her hands tightening on the nightdress. That must have been the night Jamie was conceived.

She went over to the dressing-table and got a white nightie out of the drawer, stuffing the lemon one back into it without looking at it.

Gabriel came back into the room several moments later. She was in the bed, her drained white face against the high pillows, staring at him with shadowed eyes.

Gabriel moved aside and the butler carried a bed tray into the room and placed it across the bed carefully.

'If you would rather have something different, madam——' he began as he whisked the cover off a bowl of bland chicken soup.

'No,' Marisa interrupted.

He looked at Gabriel. 'May I get you something, sir? You haven't eaten?'

Gabriel shook his head, saying nothing. Dudley inclined his head and withdrew without another word.

Marisa's nostrils quivered at the scent of the soup. Slowly she picked up the spoon. Each mouthful was an effort. She forced herself to drink half of the soup. She could not touch the golden omelette under another cover.

There were two cups on the tray and a silver pot of coffee. Marisa looked at Gabriel. 'Would you like some coffee?'

'Please.' He moved the bedroom chair to a position near the bed and sat down, crossing his long legs. She felt his proximity as a threat, her lashes flickering, but schooled herself to hide the fear he awoke in her.

Her hand shook as she handed him the cup. Gabriel shot a look at her pale face.

'Stop shaking. I'm not a monster, for God's sake.'

Marisa looked at her own cup. She did not

want the coffee, the smell of it made her feel sick, but she picked it up and sipped at it.

Gabriel drew a thick breath and leaned back, as though fighting for self-control. After a moment he drank his coffee, not looking at her. There had been so many evenings when they had sat together, not speaking, having nothing to say. Marisa had always felt the same brooding fixity in him. She felt it now. It made her mind shrivel as though at the touch of flame.

Suddenly he put down his cup, reaching a long arm across to the dressing-table to do so, and then removed her tray and placed it on the floor.

Marisa looked up, startled. Gabriel stood, his long body uncoiling so that his height made him even more alarming and impressive. The narrowed grey eyes stared down at her.

'Why?' he broke out. 'Why in God's name did you leave me?'

CHAPTER THREE

THE silence stretched between them like taut thread. Marisa had no idea what to say to him. She stared at her own hands. They were pale and cold, the fine blue veins at the wrist standing out under the smooth skin.

'I had to.'

'Why?' He sounded almost pleading, his voice husky. He was staring at her hands, too, seeing the way they trembled, the betraying tremor running through the slender fingers. 'Why won't you even tell me?'

'I tried to explain in my note.'

'That note! It told me nothing, nothing at all. How could you walk out leaving me no explanation but a few jumbled words that made no bloody sense?'

'They made sense to me,' said Marisa, clenching her hands into the sheet.

He drew a harsh breath. 'Tell me, then. Why couldn't you even talk to me face to face and explain what was wrong?'

She couldn't have talked to him. They had never talked, never communicated. They spoke the same language, but Marisa had never felt they understood each other, even when they used words they both seemed to understand. Words were only an approximation of meaning. The meaning escaped between the words, dissolved, disappeared, like fog fading away between iron bars.

When she was silent Gabriel said abruptly: 'Was there someone else?'

She started, looking up. 'No.'

He was watching her, his grey eyes hard. 'No? Who helped you get away?'

'I just walked out of the gate,' Marisa said wryly.

Gabriel moved restlessly, his face darkened with emotion. 'Taking nothing with you,' he said deeply. 'Not a thing I'd given you, not so much as a handkerchief. I came in here and you'd left it all—gone, leaving your clothes, your jewels, everything. How do you think I felt?'

'They weren't mine to take,' Marisa whispered. She had never felt she owned the presents he had given her. They had fallen all around her like a golden shower and she had shrunk back from them in disbelief.

Gabriel got up and went over to an oval pastel watercolour hanging on the wall. He pulled it forward, revealing a small wall safe, and clicked through the combination. Opening the safe, he got out a large silver box and took it over to her, flicking open the domed lid.

Marisa looked impersonally at the neatly laid out jewellery in the plush-lined drawers.

'They were yours,' said Gabriel through his teeth. 'I gave them to you. Most of them were specially made for you.'

She had never felt they were hers. They had no connection with her. They were the trappings she was expected to wear when Gabriel took her out into society as his wife. They were the insignia of her status. They outwardly demonstrated that she was the wife of Gabriel Radley, but all the time she had known inside herself that she was not his wife. She was a toy he had suddenly wanted to acquire, another possession for him to add to the vast number he already owned. From the day of their marriage Marisa had known it was not real. She had walked into a glittering nightmare and was trapped in it.

'Say something,' Gabriel ordered, flinging the silver jewellery box down on to the bed. The neat rows of jewellery were flung into disorder. Marisa slowly reached out and closed the lid on them.

'Don't you think you owed it to me to speak to me before you went away?' Gabriel demanded after a moment.

'There was nothing to say.'

'Nothing?' The word came out roughly, he bent towards her, with suppressed rage in the movement of his long body. 'You were my wife.'

Marisa looked up, her lashes flickering back from her blue eyes. 'No, that was just it. I wasn't.'

He stared, his face hardening. 'What the hell does that mean?'

'I was never your wife.'

'Don't be bloody ridiculous! What are you talking about?'

'We were married legally, but I was never really your wife.'

His smile was angry. 'Very cryptic. But what does it mean?'

'Why did you marry me?' Marisa asked in a smothered voice, looking away from the dark, angry face.

There was a little silence. 'You know why,' he said in a low, unsteady voice.

'I don't.'

'I showed you often enough.' His voice had deepened, become almost slurred, the words charged with emotion. Deliberately he bent and touched his mouth to her bare white shoulder. 'That's why,' he muttered with his lips heatedly grazing her skin.

'Don't!' she groaned, shuddering away.

He straightened, breathing thickly, his eyes flicking over her and seeing the tense stiffness of her slender body in the nightdress. His black brows jerked together and he turned away.

'If you hated to have me touch you, why did you marry me?' He stood with his back to her as he asked that, the line of his spine taut under the elegantly tailored dark suit.

Marisa had no intention of answering the question. He would misunderstand the answer.

'I made a mistake,' she whispered.

'A mistake!' He flung round, his head lifted in pain and rage, his eyes almost black as the pupil dilated and seemed to take over the paler grey of the iris.

'Yes, it was a mistake for us to get married.'

'Damn you to hell!' Gabriel grated hoarsely. He strode to the door and went out, slamming it after him.

Marisa closed her eyes, her whole body ice cold and shivering. The tension still vibrated in the silent room. Her body was being eaten alive by it.

There was a tap at the door. 'Come in,' she whispered after a pause to pull herself together.

It was second nature to her to mask what she was feeling, but her self-control was having difficulty under the present circumstances.

The butler came in softly. 'May I take your tray, madam?'

She looked at him briefly. 'Yes, thank you.'

He added Gabriel's cup to the tray and bent to lift it. Before leaving the room he said hesitantly: 'May I say how sorry we all are about the little boy, madam?'

'Thank you,' she said huskily, trying to smile. Dudley had always been kind enough in a remote, rather dry fashion. He had never made any attempt to make her feel at home in this house, but on the other hand he had always treated her with courtesy, even if the courtesy had always been distant.

'I'm sure he will be found soon.'

'Yes,' she said, because what else could she say? She did not believe the words of comfort, nor did she think Dudley believed them. Jamie was a stranger to him. He couldn't understand how she felt.

'Is there anything else I can get you, madam?'

'No, thank you,' she said, closing her eyes.

He sighed and went out, quietly shutting the door after him. Marisa looked around the room with that old sense of lost disbelief, then she switched off the bedside lamp and lay still in the darkness.

She had started work at seventeen. Her school had found her a job in London in the enormous office block which housed the Radley Corporation. She had been one of the hundreds of young girls who worked there in anonymous hordes, rushing into the building at nine and rushinng out again with relief at five-thirty. Marisa typed in a typing pool, her desk cheek by jowl with that of the girl next to her, their day supervised by a slim, elegant young woman in a black dress. She always wore black. She wasn't married, but the girls called her the Black Widow among themselves and disliked her intensely. She was sarcastic and sharp-tongued and ran the typing pool like a piece of clockwork.

Marisa did not have much trouble at work. She was quiet and subdued and always did what she was told. A model employee. After six months she was sufficiently trusted to be moved out of the typing pool and sent as a typist to work in one of the smaller, upper offices attached to the high executives in the corporation.

The work was basically the same, but there were fewer people around her and she had more variety in what she did. She also earned more.

She left home and got a bedsitting-room where she would have more privacy and freedom.

She was not the type of girl who attracts attention from men. Slender, reserved, a shy introvert, she ran from any overt interest shown to her by the men she worked with at the corporation.

She was trying to find her feet in London. A great city is an easy place to get lost in, and Marisa was already a girl who felt herself to be under threat from the unreal and impersonal nature of the world.

Her childhood had left her with a haunting sense of impermanence. She was afraid to let herself feel safe because she had a permanent, helpless fear of loss. Although she never rationalised it to herself she believed that if she loved something or someone it would vanish, be taken away from her. Everything had. All her life people, places and things had vanished. She had never even had a doll she could call her own. When they moved somehow her things always seemed to get lost. Her parents barely seemed to remember to take her with them. They would look at her in surprise as though wondering who she was, her existence some sort of afterthought which they had difficulty in remembering.

They loved each other with such absorbed intensity that a third party was neither wanted nor needed. They were both silent people. They did not talk much, even to each other, but they seemed to understand each other without words. Marisa had made an uneasy third in that household all her life until at last she made up her mind to leave it. Her parents showed no surprise or concern. She suspected they were relieved.

Her bedsitting-room was impermanent, too. It was furnished in a dull, shabby fashion with things probably bought at a sale. They were ugly and old and had belonged to a series of people, judging by the condition of them. Marisa did not so much live there as exist within the ugly shell.

She had begun to explore London in her spare time. There was always something to do in London, but Marisa was always alone and always aware of the pressing mass of other human beings with whom she had no contact and no shared sense of community.

When she was nineteen, she joined the string of secretaries working in Gabriel Radley's enormous office. She never saw him at close quarters. He strode through the office without pausing to give so much as a glance at any of the secretaries. They might as well have been machines. They talked about him, of course, and knew great quantities of facts about his private life. Every mention of him in a newspaper was noted and discussed. It was a matter of pride to most of them that they worked directly under him, although he never spoke to them, all his orders coming down through a chain of command which ended in the woman who ran the secretarial side of the office.

Gabriel was one of the jet-set. He flew across the Atlantic so often that it was like commuting to him. He had his own planes and one of them was always waiting for him if he suddenly chose to dash off to some other part of the world.

Marisa barely thought about him, except to recognise the gulf between the world in which he lived and the one which she inhabited. She could not even imagine what it must be like to be Gabriel Radley, to know that you were the most important person in that great office block, to walk in and out of planes as though they were subways, to never have to think about money because it was something you had always had. The fixed realities of her life were a weekly struggle to feed herself, clothe herself, pay her rent. She saw Gabriel through a glass, darkly, hardly believing him to be real. He was as much a myth to her as the shadowy figures she saw on film when she visited the cinema on the rare occasions she could afford it.

One Monday morning she was late for work. Hurrying towards the office in pelting rain, she dived towards the swing doors, eager to get under cover, and ran full tilt into Gabriel as he came out of them. He steadied her, his sinewy hands grabbing her shoulders, and she looked up into his face, startled.

Gabriel had stared into the enormous, confused blue eyes for a few seconds, then he had said curtly: 'Look where you're going unless you want to have an accident,' releasing her as he spoke and turning away.

Marisa had gone on into the building, oddly

disturbed by the narrowed inspecting stare he had given her. In the cloakroom she had stared at herself in the mirror above the washbasins. Her hair had been damp, curling around her temples, the plastic rain hood she wore leaving only the front of her head bare. Her face had looked pale, shadowy, her eyes full of nervous puzzlement.

What was puzzling her was her own reaction. Gabriel Radley meant nothing to her except as the man who ultimately paid her weekly wage. But she could still feel the long hands clamping her shoulders, the skin where he had touched her burning.

He was not seen in the office for several days. 'Flew to New York yesterday,' some more knowledgeable girl said.

'To see Capri,' someone said, and they all giggled.

Gabriel's romances made part of their private mythology. They tracked them in newspapers and magazines, gazing at photographs of beautiful women with scathing criticism.

'I can't see what he sees in *her*. She won't last long,' they would decide, dismissing some long-legged, glossy blonde with a sniff.

The latest woman in his well-publicised life was Capri Gardien, a French-born, Hollywood-manufactured actress whose name was better known than her films. Svelte, sophisticated, she was always being photographed in low-cut evening gowns or minute bikinis, her acting ability less important than her superb figure and the wild, copper-coloured hair which blew around her face.

'Isn't he married?' Marisa asked one morning. It was the first time she had ever shown any interest in Gabriel and the others all looked at her, delighted to demonstrate their knowledge of his private life.

'He was once.' Karen leaned forward, tapping a pink fingernail on her desk, as one of the others tried to speak. 'I'll tell her. You mean you don't know? Really? It's terrible.'

'It must have been awful for him,' another girl said.

'What?' Marisa asked.

'His wife and his little boy were killed, ambushed by terrorists in South America. They were all visiting his wife's family. She was South American and they were very rich, some sort of cattle barons, wasn't it?'

'Factories,' someone said. 'They had factories, didn't they?'

'No, it was cattle and they packed the meat in their own factories,' Karen said impatiently. 'Well, the car they were driving was ambushed and in the fighting the whole family were killed. Gabriel wasn't with them. He was supposed to be, but he'd flown off back to England that day, otherwise he would have been killed, too.'

Marisa had absorbed the information with a shock. She had not imagined that Gabriel Radley's life would have anything so violent or tragic in it. He had seemed so impervious, his world one of shiny cars and fast planes, beautiful women and power. The story about his wife and child brought him into sharper focus for her, made him a human being who had been hurt.

When he appeared again in London she saw him walking through the office with a curious sensation of familiarity. He did not notice her, of course. He was striding along with a string of men at his heels, throwing curt remarks to them over his shoulder, and they were all smiling as though the slightest thing he said was somehow riveting.

'Creeps,' Karen muttered, glaring after them. 'Look at the way they scurry after him! He scares them stiff.'

He scared Marisa. He was so tall and so powerful, his expensive formal suits unable to mute the physical strength of that long body, his muscled shoulders straining under the smooth cloth.

He had had a sports club built down in the bowels of the building. Employees could play squash, swim, work off surplus energy in the superbly equipped gymnasium. Some of the girls went down there once a week. Marisa rarely accompanied them. She found it hard to make friends with people. She couldn't think of anything to say, her shyness almost a wall between herself and everyone she met.

A fortnight after the rainy morning when she had run into him she went down to the sports club to play squash. An office tournament had been arranged by Karen, who was a great organiser and bullied everyone in sight into taking part in one of her schemes.

'I'm not very good at squash,' Marisa had protested, her face a little pink.

'None of us are, but that doesn't stop us enjoying a game,' said Karen, dismissing her attempt to get out of it. 'Anyway, I need you to make up the numbers. At least you can play, you're not a total dud.'

Marisa found it hard to argue with Karen. There was a cheerful ruthlessness about the other girl which floored Marisa every time. Karen bulldozed her way through life, smiling widely, ignoring what anybody else said or thought. Tall, blonde, freckle-faced, she was fond of sport and very good at all athletic pastimes, so that she refused to believe that what she liked and found so easy could be hard or unattractive to anybody else.

Changing in the shower rooms, Marisa wandered along the cream-painted corridor to look for the squash court she was playing on in ten minutes. A door opened and Gabriel Radley strode out. He halted to allow Marisa to pass him, and she lowered her eyes, slightly flushed. He walked behind her until she went into the squash court. It was empty. Her partner had not yet arrived and nobody was using the court, so Marisa started practising. She was an active girl but not a powerful one. She played better tennis than squash.

Turning to pick up the ball, her short white

skirt swinging, she found Gabriel Radley standing in the doorway, watching her. Marisa's heart
plunged oddly as though she was on a fairground
dipper. When she straightened from picking up
the ball her face was very hct.

The room was empty again. Gabriel had gone.
Marisa stared at the place where he had stood,
wondering what had brought him in here, and
why he had stared at her in that odd, narrowed
way.

She played her game very badly and lost hands
down. Karen gave her a contemptuous smile.
'Well, you tried,' she said, adding, 'I suppose.'

Marisa took a shower and dressed again. As she
came out of the office building a car slid up from
the underground car park. Marisa walked along
the crowded pavement to the nearest crossing. A
moment later the sleek limousine was pulling up
beside her. Startled, she looked at the man in the
back of it. He had wound down the window.

'Get in,' he said coolly, opening the door.

Marisa looked around, flustered, not believing
he meant her, and met curious stares from the
other people waiting for the lights to change.
They changed at that moment and people began
to surge across the road.

'Get in,' Gabriel Radley repeated in an impati-
ent voice, and when she just stared, dumb-
founded, at him, added: 'Please.'

Marisa got into the car, so nervous that she
banged her head as she climbed in beside him.
The door closed and the car drew away. Marisa

swallowed and looked at Gabriel hesitantly. What on earth did he want?

It never occurred to her to imagine that his intentions might be extremely personal. She had seen the sort of women Gabriel Radley could whistle up when he felt like female company. Marisa knew that she was not beautiful. She was shy, unsophisticated and very young. She was puzzled by what was happening, but she imagined that Gabriel had some reason for inviting her to join him in the car.

He leaned back beside her, watching her, his black head flung back against the upholstery in a relaxed fashion. 'What's your name?'

'Marisa,' she said softly.

He did not ask for her surname. He repeated: 'Marisa,' in a slow voice. His usual voice was the one she had heard in the office, from a distance, the deep curt tones commanding, but now it murmured like hazy smoke, his straight lips scarcely parting to say her name.

'Where do you live? We'll drive you home,' he added. 'I want to talk to you.'

She hesitated, then gave him the address and he relayed it to the driver, who nodded his peaked cap towards them in the driving mirror.

Gabriel glanced back at her. 'I saw you in the sports club. Do you use it often? What do you think of it? I had a lot of opposition when I first suggested it—some of the board thought it a ridiculous idea. What do you think? Is it popular with the staff?'

Marisa smiled in unconscious relief, realising why he had stopped to offer her a lift. 'I don't use it much myself, but a lot of the others do. I'd say it was very popular.'

'Are the facilities adequate? Or was there some sport that didn't occur to me?'

'I think you thought of everything,' Marisa said a little drily, remembering all the expensive modern sports equipment.

While she was speaking he was staring at her, his grey eyes intent, moving in a restless way from her eyes to her mouth and back again.

'How old are you?' he asked in an abrupt voice.

'Nineteen,' she said, and saw his black brows jerk together. For some reason she hurriedly added: 'Nearly twenty.'

He laughed shortly, giving her a sardonic look. 'Nearly twenty? Yes, that makes a hell of a difference to nineteen.'

Marisa couldn't see why she should feel she ought to apologise for her age, nor why Gabriel should be frowning heavily as he glanced away from her and stared out of the window.

'I was married when I was twenty,' he said, taking her entirely by surprise. He didn't look round, his wide shoulders thrust back in an odd sort of movement which spoke of silent defiance, a shrug towards some thought inside himself.

Marisa was silent, not knowing what to say, thinking of his dead wife and child with sadness. He glanced at her, his eyes probing her face.

'You know about that,' he stated flatly.

Marisa met his stare, her lower lip caught between her teeth, struggling to find a way of expressing her sympathy but too shy and uncertain to know what to say. In the end she just nodded, trying to convey her feelings with a shy little smile.

'Haven't much to say for yourself, have you?' Gabriel muttered. 'But those eyes say a lot.' He flicked a hand up to her face, one finger brushing her cheek. 'I've never seen such eyes on anyone. They're unforgettable.'

Marisa's colour glowed heatedly under her usually pale skin and he watched the invasion with acute observation, his eyes narrowing.

'Do you live with your family?' he asked.

She shook her head. 'I've got a room in a bedsit house.'

His brows rose. 'Rather lonely for you. Where do your family live?'

'Blackheath.'

'Couldn't you commute from there? It's an easy enough journey.'

'I prefer to live alone,' Marisa explained, a sudden wry smile twisting her mouth. Gabriel watched it with that probing curiosity, looking up into her eyes as though to check their expression too.

'You don't get on with your family? Is it a big one?'

'No, just my parents.'

'You're an only child?' He watched her nod and said: 'Yes, you look like an only child.'

'How do they look?' Marisa was half amused, half dubious.

'Self-sufficient, defensive, wary,' he said. 'I should know, I'm one myself. Loneliness can become a habit and habits aren't easy to break.' He shot her a brief look. 'Are you lonely? Or have you got a boy-friend?'

Her colour rose again. Before she could answer the car had stopped outside the house in which she lived. She saw Gabriel glance out, saw the wry face he made at the shabby old house.

'This is it?'

She nodded, reaching for the doorhandle, muttering a polite word of gratitude for the lift. Gabriel shifted, putting his hand over hers, making every nerve in her body leap as though touched by fire. Marisa looked up at him, shaken.

'Hang on a minute,' he said brusquely. 'You didn't answer my question. Have you got a boy-friend?'

She shook her head dumbly, looking down. Gabriel released her hand and she found the door opening. Stumbling out on to the pavement, she heard the door close again and then the sleek vehicle accelerated away.

She stared after it in dazed confusion. The whole incident was so unbelievable. What strange impulse had made Gabriel Radley pick her up and drive her home, ask her all those questions? Had he been bored, at a loose end, restless? The obvious answer with almost anybody else could have been a desire for a casual evening's entertainment, but Marisa wasn't the sort of girl whose appearance immediately put thoughts of that sort into a man's head. She walked into the house and let herself into her room. In the dressing-table mirror she stared at herself, trying to see any reason for Gabriel Radley's peculiar interest in her.

Slender, delicate, usually pale, her straight black hair framed her face and emphasised the physical fragility of her fine bones. Her only asset was her eyes. Huge, beautifully formed, they dominated her face, but they certainly did not account for what had just happened. Marisa shrugged. The explanation had to be mere impulse. She would never see Gabriel Radley again except at a distance.

She was wrong. A few days later she was informed that Gabriel wanted to see her. 'You made an error in that South African list of stocks,' she was told irritably. 'Mr Radley is annoyed. He asked who'd typed it and now he wants to see you himself. Why weren't you more careful?'

He had known who had typed it before he asked. Her initials were always typed at the top of the account sheet alongside those of the man responsible for the original figures.

Marisa went into the office and Gabriel leaned back in his chair, his jacket open and one hand plucking at the pocket of his waistcoat.

'There's a mistake in these figures. You've lost ten thousand pounds somewhere.'

'I'm sorry, sir,' Marisa said quietly. 'I'll do them again.'

She reached for the paper and he put his hand quite deliberately on top of hers.

She stiffened, looking at his hand. The dark hair and sinewy strength of it completely swallowed the slender pallor of her own.

'Have dinner with me,' he said deeply.

She looked up, her heart jumping about inside her chest as if it was a frog.

'Please,' he muttered. His cheeks carried a dark red stain of colour and a muscle jerked beside his mouth.

'Why?' Marisa asked in a bewildered, soft voice.

'Because I'm going out of my mind,' Gabriel said through his teeth. 'I've got to see you.'

She couldn't believe him. The harsh, driven sound of his voice carried its own conviction, but it seemed so unbelievable. Marisa shook her head, pulling her hand from under his and backing away from the desk in a nervous haste which betrayed her fear.

He got up and came round the desk in three strides. Before she got to the door he was in front of her, leaning against it, staring at her with those darkened eyes.

'There's nothing you can say that I haven't already said to myself. It's lunacy, but you've haunted me ever since I set eyes on you that day in the rain. I flew to New York and everywhere I looked I saw your huge blue eyes. I came home and there you were in my outer office, typing like a demure little mouse, never looking up when I walked past, ignoring me. I can't count the number of times I've walked through that room completely unnecessarily just to see your head bent over the typewriter. You never looked at me once.'

The rapid, muttered words sank into her mind and made no sense. She moistened her lips nervously and he looked at her quickly.

'Yes?' he asked, almost pleading for her to say something.

Marisa shook her head, dumb.

'I've got to see you, talk to you, be with you. You've hit me like a runaway truck and I can't think of anything else.' He put a hand to her face, caressing her pale cheek. 'Have dinner with me.'

'I can't,' Marisa refused.

'That's all I want,' said Gabriel. 'Just dinner. I'm not planning to try to talk you into bed. I only want to find out what you're like under that haunting little face.'

She wavered, staring at him.

'Please,' he whispered, smiling, and the smile made up her mind for her. It was crooked, self-deriding, faintly pleading. It made his whole face look different. It made Marisa's heart turn over.

They had dinner at a quiet London restaurant. Marisa was nervous because her dress seemed so much less elegant than those the other female customers were wearing. Gabriel barely glanced at it. He sat talking to her, watching her face

every second of the time, his eyes flickering up to
hers or dropping to the pink curve of her mouth.

He asked her all about her family background,
about her school, her friends, her interests. There
was so little Marisa could tell him. She was so
ordinary, so far outside his life style, his friends.
What on earth did a man with his money and gla-
morous existence see in a girl of nineteen who
had never been anywhere, done anything, had
neither money nor charm and was so shy she had
to force herself to look up at him from time to
time?

Normally her eyes were fixed on the table, her
lashes flickering, her ears strained to catch his
soft questions. Every now and again she looked at
him, though, and selfconsciously looked away
when their eyes met.

Over their coffee Gabriel moved the candle
which was between them so that it no longer
shielded her at all, casting a dark little shadow on
the cloth instead. While she was listening to him
Marisa began tracing the outline of the shadow
and Gabriel moved his hand gently until his
fingers just touched her own. Her heart thudded.
She did not look up, watching as he brushed his
fingertips along hers, drew one finger lightly over
her palm.

It was at that moment that she began to believe
that Gabriel meant what he had said. His tentative, gentle caress altered the whole feel of their
relationship.

He did not try to kiss her that evening. He

drove her home himself, and said goodnight softly, waiting until she had let herself into the house before driving away.

Two nights later she had dinner with him again. Gabriel did most of the talking, but in fact even he did not speak very much. They were both intent, their voices low, their eyes fixed on the table in the strange nervous fixity of people undergoing an intense attraction when it is in its first stages.

He kissed her in the car outside her house. When he drew her towards him Marisa felt her heart racing so fast that she felt sick. She yielded her mouth hesitantly. She had never been kissed before in her life, and she had no idea what to do. She lay in his arms, her soft mouth quivering, and Gabriel gave a sudden hoarse groan and began to kiss her with absorbed hunger. She made no attempt to kiss him back. Her surrender was not matched by any passion inside herself. Her excitement was half fear, her yielding half unexpressed resistance.

A week later Gabriel asked her to marry him. Marisa was thrown into panic. She did not know why she was so scared, but the idea of being his wife petrified her.

'I can't,' she had moaned, scrambling out of the car.

Gabriel followed her, caught her arm, his fingers biting into her. 'Why not? Why not?' he had demanded. 'Is there anybody else?'

'No,' Marisa had denied angrily. 'But I

couldn't marry you.'

'Why not?'

'I'm not from your world,' she said, shivering.

His face had become a hard, determined mask. She saw ferocity in the grey eyes, a decisive intention. 'I don't give a damn what you are or who you are. I want you—I've got to have you. I won't let you say no to me, Marisa. Until you're mine I'm not going to have a moment's peace.'

It had taken him a few more weeks to wear down her frightened, bewildered, disturbed resistance. Their marriage was a nine days' wonder. Marisa had moved through it like a zombie, finding the whole thing too appalling to bear, yet too scared of Gabriel's tenacity by now to argue with him. Her parents came to the wedding but had no part in the arrangements. Marisa and Gabriel had driven over to their house in Blackheath to explain that the wedding had to be so large-scale that it would be best if Gabriel's staff did all the organising. The gulf between Marisa and her mother meant that there was no way she could discuss her worries about the marriage. She had no one in whom she could confide. She had nowhere to run to even if she plucked up the courage to run.

Gabriel was rushing her into marriage at top speed, with the fanatic insistence of a man under the grip of a violent emotion.

Their honeymoon in Bermuda was a surrealist dream to Marisa. She couldn't believe in the lush, tropical surroundings or the heated sensual passion Gabriel showed her. She lay in his arms at night with confused incredulity.

While they were there they got word that Marisa's parents had been killed in a collision with a lorry. Marisa did not cry. She took the news in shattered silence. They flew back for the funeral. It was a cold, dry day with a livid sky stretching above the cemetery as the funeral took place. Marisa looked up into the empty air and shivered. She felt totally alone.

That sense of isolation grew over the next months. Gabriel had to spend long stretches of time away from her. She felt cut off from life in the huge, elegant alien house. She did not know how to cope with the servants, the visitors, the people from Gabriel's old life who looked at his pale, slender young wife with a mixture of pity and distaste. She realised, although it was never said in her presence, that most of his friends regarded her as some sort of manic impulse on Gabriel's part, a sudden piece of folly from which he would one day awake.

She believed it was true, herself. Gabriel was so rich that he had always acquired what he wanted. His houses were stuffed full of beautiful objects. His sleek cars filled several garages. If he saw something he liked he bought it, without even stopping to think whether or not he really needed it.

Marisa felt she was one of the objects he had bought and which he handled with caressing enjoyment whenever he had nothing more important to do. They couldn't talk to each other; they had nothing to say. They did not know each other. They had nothing in common. The only thing they could do was make love, and this one fragile bridge could not take too much weight. It would snap, she realised, once Gabriel was sexually tired of her.

They began to quarrel. Because their relationship had largely a physical basis their quarrels were sudden and violent. Marisa found herself saying bitter, stinging things which she would never have imagined she could say once.

She refused to have a child. At the back of her mind she could not forget Gabriel's first wife and the boy who had been killed with her, and she was afraid that any child she had would die, too. The impermanence of life which she had always felt so deeply had been underlined for her by the deaths of her parents and by that memory of Gabriel's first wife.

She couldn't put it into words when Gabriel challenged her. She tried to explain how she felt, but fear stifled the words.

Gabriel did not understand about her private terrors, the nightmares which were haunting her sleep at night. He only understood that she had been reluctant to marry him, was reluctant to bear his child.

During one bitter row he had slapped her, his hand leaving a red stain on her cheek when she'd flung some angry accusation at him. Marisa had been left totally bereft after that, because it made

her see Gabriel as a self-obsessed stranger who regarded her as yet another of his possessions but
one that had the temerity to try to think for itself.

Gabriel was gone when she woke up next
morning. She was told he had flown to New
York. A newspaper a few days later told her that
he had been seen at a nightclub in the company
of Capri Gardien. Marisa drew her own conclu-
sions. She wrote him a brief cold note and on a
pretext of going shopping she escaped the super-
vision of her chauffeur and vanished into the
crowded isolation of London.

She had had some vague, unrealised idea of
spending her life in bitter loneliness. When she
thought ahead to the future that was the picture
she saw. All that was changed by Jamie's arrival.
He had plugged her into life and made her real at
last, giving her life some shape and purpose,
colouring the world around her in a totally new
way.

Marisa lay in the dark room trying to sleep but
knowing that she would not sleep, remembering a
past which was almost entirely bitter until Jamie
came to give her hope.

She had always been so afraid that fate would
reach out to destroy whatever she loved.

She had run from Gabriel's silken house and
iron possession only to wind up back here again,
facing the possibility that she was never again
going to see the one person in the world she had
ever loved with a whole, undivided, secure heart
and who had had the same love to give her.

Jamie's smile when she picked him up in the mornings, the warm clutch of his plump arms round her neck, his chuckle when something amused him, his stamping roar when something annoyed him—all came flooding back to make her heart wince.

'Jamie, Jamie,' she whispered into the unheeding darkness, 'where are you?'

CHAPTER FOUR

SHE opened her eyes to find the room full of light. Blinking, she adjusted her thoughts and the memory of Jamie rushed back at her. She sat up, a stifled cry on her lips, and found Gabriel at the foot of the bed watching her.

'Oh!' she gasped, shrinking.

'Don't look like that!'

Marisa bit her lip, looking down, then looked up. 'Jamie? Is there any news?'

He slowly shook his head, the movement reluctant, his hard face filled with unexpressed emotion.

Marisa's body slackened in silent grief and she put her hands over her eyes. 'Why can't somebody find him?'

'They will,' said Gabriel, moving.

She saw him through her spread fingers as he sat down on the edge of the bed. Tentatively he touched her arm, moving his fingertips down the smooth pale skin.

'No news is sometimes good news.' It was a dull cliché, but there was the slight tinge of truth to it. While they had no news of Jamie at least they could hope. Marisa was ready to clutch at any straw.

There was a newspaper on the end of the bed.

77

Gabriel picked it up and laid it out in front of her, flattening it on the quilt. 'They must have got it from the people you've been living with,' he said, jerking a long finger at the photograph taking up most of the front page.

Marisa's heart stopped and she looked at the picture of Jamie with tears stinging behind her eyes. She remembered the day she had taken it, the enormous grin with which Jamie had gazed at her while Sally held his hand. Jamie was laughing in the picture, his curly head thrown back, his sturdy little body dressed in white trousers and a shirt printed with elephants.

'He looks like you,' she murmured. Jamie liked his own way, too. He hadn't grown up with a silver spoon in his mouth. Marisa had had to be careful with money. But Jamie knew what he wanted, all the same, and went for it with the same unswerving insistence Gabriel could show.

'Does he?' Gabriel sounded husky, staring at the photograph as though trying to see some resemblance.

'His colouring is different, but the shape of his face, the way he looks, reminds me . . .' She broke off, biting her lip, fighting to hold back tears.

'The press had picked up the background,' Gabriel grated, his face darkening as his eyes moved on to the story printed around the picture. 'I'm afraid it's causing a storm of interest. It's always news when a baby is snatched, but my baby makes it a sensation.'

'Someone may recognise him, though,' Marisa

thought aloud. 'People will see the picture and may remember something.' Surely it would help to find Jamie? He had to be somewhere. Someone had to have seen him.

'How could you keep him away from me all these months?' Gabriel erupted in a deep, harsh angry voice. 'He's my son. How could you do it?'

Her lips trembled. There had been so many reasons why she had kept Jamie's birth a secret. She hadn't wanted to go back to Gabriel. She had dreaded the idea of becoming a doll in a luxurious doll's house again. But she had known that if Gabriel knew about Jamie he would want his son. He would have moved heaven and earth to take possession of him.

Everything she ever loved had been taken away. She had clung to Jamie with fevered determination.

'Why don't you ever talk to me?' Gabriel demanded, staring at her with leaping grey eyes. 'Every time I ask a question you just stare at me with those vague blue eyes. I thought once that I could find out what went on behind those eyes, but you defeat me at every turn. You've never once tried to move out towards me, have you, Marisa? You keep me at a distance and won't let me get near you.'

She wanted to tell him that she was afraid, afraid of the day when Gabriel tired of her. She couldn't risk the pain he would give her if she let herself surrender entirely. Gabriel had married her because he was in the grip of a burning, obsessive passion. She had been forced to believe in that passion, but she had never believed it had either depth or future. Obsessions die. Marisa could not risk trusting to Gabriel's love for her.

'Couldn't you even have let me know you were safe?' Gabriel asked abruptly, his fingers closing round her arm. 'Do you have any idea what I went through when I came back here and found you'd just vanished? I combed London for you. I had detectives searching everywhere I could think of. Did you change your name?'

'No,' she said, shaking her head. That hadn't occurred to her. She had felt so safe in the anonymous suburb of London where she had found a home. There were so many people living around her, an unknown sea of human beings, their names and faces outside her knowledge. She had felt hidden, safe, a leaf hanging in the middle of a wood. Somehow she had known Gabriel would not find her. How many people in London were named Radley? And as she had expected, he had half supposed she would change her name if she wanted to stay lost.

He was staring at her profile, the pale subdued outline turned towards him. 'You look older,' he commented.

'I am older.'

'Different,' he said.

'I've had a child. That changes people.' It was more than the physical change. Jamie had altered the whole world for her. Love did that. It was a kaleidoscope, shaking the jumbled pieces of life up and letting them fall in a new, delightful pattern.

'And me?' he asked harshly. 'Am I different? I'm older, two years older. I'll soon be forty and you'll only be twenty-five.'

Marisa could not dispute that. They were facts. She could tell him that it made no difference at all to how she felt. His age had never meant a thing to her. It wouldn't have mattered if he had been the same age as herself if she had been able to believe he loved her and would always love her.

But she couldn't believe that. She scratched at the quilt cover with one finger, her head bent.

'And for nearly two years I've been a father again without knowing a damn thing about it!'

She thought of his first child and lifted her head to look at him sadly. 'I'm sorry about your other son. And your wife. I always wanted to say I was sorry, but it never came out.'

He looked at her in grim assessment. 'I thought you were jealous. Were you?'

She shook her head. 'No.' Then added honestly, 'I don't think so. You never mentioned her. Them.'

'I didn't want to remind you of anything in the past,' Gabriel said. 'It made the age gap seem wider.'

'I thought it might be because you couldn't bear to talk about them.'

He shrugged, the strong lines of his face set. 'I can't say I enjoy remembering. Dolores and I

were in love when we got married, but she started
having other men after a couple of years. She
didn't like Europe. She felt more at home in
South America. It was where she grew up and
she liked the social life there. We spent a lot of
time apart. Paul was born a year after we
married, but I saw very little of him. Dolores
took him around with her all the time. He had a
nanny, but Dolores wanted Paul with her, so I
scarcely knew him.' He paused. 'He was only six
when he was killed.'

The curt words made her body shrivel in pain.
She whitened and Gabriel gave a low groan,
taking her into his arms.

'Don't, we'll find Jamie. Don't look like that.'

She felt so frightened and sick that she leant on
him, all her weight falling on his wide strong
shoulder. She heard the steady living beat of his
heart under her cheek and then his lips smoothing the dark strands of hair at her temples.

'I'm so scared,' she whispered.

'I know.' He was softly stroking down her
spine, the palm of his hand warm against her
body.

'Jamie's so little.'

'Ssh!' Gabriel slid his mouth down her hair,
breathing quickly. Marisa was too absorbed in
her own pain and fear to be aware of his emotions, her slender body trembling in his arms.

Gabriel was so strong. His body had a driving
purpose which had once terrified her but which
in this moment of weakness made her feel safe.

The rhythm of his heart had altered, quickened. The hand moving up and down her back wasn't quite steady. She felt his lips touching her ear, tracing the curve of it delicately.

'You're so tiny and delicate,' he muttered. 'You look as if you could break in half if someone handled you roughly. That was the first thing that struck me about you—how fragile you were. I wanted to hold you like this and know that you were mine.'

The thickly muttered words disturbed her, broke her out of the safe trance in which his caresses had held her. She pulled away, flushing, striking his hand away.

'Don't!'

Gabriel's face darkened with angry colour. His eyes flashed and savagery hardened the line of his mouth. 'Don't push me away like that!'

'I don't want you to touch me.'

Rage broke out in him, his body tense with it, his eyes burning on her. 'You little bitch, I don't give a damn what you want! You've driven me crazy for two years, wondering where you were, who you were with, what was happening to you, and then you calmly tell me you don't want me to touch you! I could kill you, do you know that?'

She believed him. The unleashed fury inside him showed in his whole darkened face, the blood burning under his skin and his hands shaking with temper.

She faced him, terrified but determined not to show it, her chin lifted defiantly. 'You made me come back here. I didn't want to come. I'm not staying. And I don't want your hands on me!'

Gabriel's mouth twisted in furious bitterness 'That's too bad,' he muttered deep in his throat. 'Because you're going to get my hands on you and like it!'

His hands fell on her with a strength which stripped away her brief flare of courage. Gasping, she was pulled against him and her lips were crushed under his, the punitive bitter kiss giving no pleasure, only hurting and compelling.

One hand grasped the back of her head, his fingers grabbing her loose black hair, dragging her head back to enforce his possession of her mouth.

She had no hope of escape. The fury in him relived for her the night when his anger had exploded and he had struck her and left her alone and weeping. Gabriel's chaotic, volcanic emotion had always been beyond her comprehension. She did not know how to fight against it, how to understand it. Whatever her imagination had made of love she had never expected it to be a bitter obsessive desire which refused to be denied.

Breathing thickly, he raised his head. The leaping grey eyes stared into her own. Swallowing, he muttered: 'You forced me to do that. I can't stand it when you push me away. Are you blind that you don't know what you do to me?'

Her mouth was shaking. It felt hot and swollen where he had crushed it under his, the inner lip tender.

Gabriel closed his eyes. 'Oh, God, I'm sorry—I didn't mean to do that. I lost my temper. You drove me out of my mind. Having you in my arms again, touching you, the scent of your skin all round me, and then having you push me away. I've woken up a hundred times in the past two years from dreams like this and felt like smashing everything in the house.'

'You hurt me,' Marisa whispered, touching her burning mouth with one finger.

'I'm sorry,' he muttered. 'Marisa . . .'

There was a tap at the door, and Gabriel gave an exclamation, getting up in a rapid, angry movement. 'Yes?'

Dudley looked at him impassively from the door. 'There is someone to see you, sir.'

'Not now, for God's sake,' Gabriel grated.

Dudley did not move, but his eyes looked at Gabriel with silent meaning. 'I think you should come, sir.'

Gabriel stiffened. 'Very well,' he said, after a brief pause. Marisa stared at Dudley, her heart thudding. She sensed that this was something to do with Jamie.

'What is it?' she faltered.

Dudley glanced at her, his face calm. 'A gentleman to see Mr Radley, madam, that's all.'

Gabriel strode towards the door and both men went out. Marisa flew out of the bed and fumbled to find a dressing gown. The first she found hanging in the fitted wardrobe was a lacy white confection with soft angora collar and hem. She pulled it on hurriedly and followed Gabriel downstairs.

The hall was empty. The mellow tones of the

grandfather clock chimed the quarter hour. Marisa heard voices in the library and stood at the door, listening, uncertain whether to go in or not. It might genuinely be a business matter. Only instinct warned her that this was connected with Jamie's disappearance, and she might have been mistaken in her suspicion that Dudley was hiding something from her.

'How much are they asking?' Gabriel was demanding, his voice harsh.

'Fifty thousand.'

'What? Only that much?'

'My thoughts exactly, sir,' the other voice said, very softly. 'Curious, isn't it?'

'Is it a try-on?'

'At this stage it is hard to say. That did occur to me.'

'Was there any proof it was genuine?' Gabriel's voice wasn't quite steady. 'It was a phone call? No tape, no pictures?'

'Just a phone call, no proof of any kind. If it's genuine, that will come later, and if it's genuine the price will go up.'

'Steeply,' Gabriel grated.

The other voice was calm. 'I would say so. If it's professional. With amateurs you can never tell.'

'You think it may be an amateur?'

'It's a very odd way of doing it. The whole thing is odd. It looks to me like an impulse snatch. Only when they found out who the child was did they think of money.'

Marisa's body was stiff and cold. She put her hand on the door, but before she had pushed it open, Gabriel said: 'I don't want this to get to my wife—she's in a state of shock. Can we keep it out of the papers?'

Marisa opened the door and Gabriel pivoted, his face whitening as he met her angry blue eyes.

'I heard,' Marisa said starkly. She looked at the policeman, who was observing her closely in silence. He had a calm, impassive face which hid secrets but was always watchful, the colourless eyes flickering over her from her loose, flowing black hair to her white negligee, most of his attention given to her face, probing it in an attempt to judge her character.

'What has happened?'

'There has been a phone call to a newspaper,' Gabriel said, moving towards her. 'Sit down, Marisa.' He touched her arm tentatively, not quite sure how she was going to react.

'Jamie's all right? Did they say he was all right?' She stared at the other man pleadingly. 'What did they say about Jamie?'

'Sit down, Marisa,' Gabriel begged.

'Leave me alone,' she broke out, her voice shaking. 'What did they tell you about Jamie?' She pushed Gabriel away, keeping her eyes fixed on the other man.

'We aren't sure yet whether the phone call is genuine,' he said. 'It may be, but on the other hand, after all the publicity, it's quite common to get phone calls from nutters who are just out to make trouble, and my instinct tells me that this is a time-waster.'

'But if it is . . .' she began.

'If it's genuine I'll pay the ransom,' Gabriel interrupted. 'We'll get Jamie back if it costs me every penny I've got.'

'It's always a mistake to pay them,' the policeman said flatly. 'The first bite merely makes them greedy for more.'

'I'm not taking risks with my son's life,' Gabriel blazed, his grey eyes hard and angry.

The other man shrugged. 'I can't stop you paying the money over, sir, but I advise against it. In my experience . . .'

'We'll pay,' said Gabriel, cutting him short with a straight, deadly look which held a warning.

'What?' Marisa asked, fear clutching at her. 'What were you going to say?'

'Nothing,' Gabriel said in a grim voice. 'Just hold on to the belief that we're going to get Jamie back, no matter what it costs. The money's irrelevant.'

The policeman shrugged again, giving Marisa a quick exploratory glance. 'As you say, sir, but may I ask you to co-operate with us all the way? Even if you're going to pay the money we want to be kept fully informed of any approaches made to you. The wire tap has been set up, and any direct approach to you will be monitored. Whatever happens, don't hide things from us. Kidnapping is a serious crime and you would only be encouraging them to do it again if you help them to get away with it this time.'

'What were you going to say earlier?' Marisa repeated as he stopped speaking. 'Something about in your experience?'

The man looked at Gabriel, who closed his eyes and sighed. Quietly the policeman said: 'In my experience kidnappers rarely keep their promises.'

'Meaning what?' Marisa asked, although she was already guessing what he meant and trembling violently.

'Even if you pay, you won't necessarily get your son back,' he told her quite gently.

She sagged, her face entirely bloodless, and Gabriel gave a low exclamation, catching her in his arms, her heavy head drooping against his shoulder. Gabriel looked at the policeman with murderous rage.

'Why the hell couldn't you keep your mouth shut?' He lifted Marisa into his arms and carried her out of the room, her white robe trailing behind them.

Gabriel laid her down on her bed and moved away. She was stirring as he bent over her, a glass of water in his hand. Her lashes lifted and the great blue eyes stared at him, glazed with fear.

'What are we going to do?'

'Whatever we have to do,' said Gabriel, sitting down beside her on the bed and sliding an arm under her head to lift her, strands of black hair floating over his dark sleeve.

He put the glass to her lips and she sipped, coughing as some of the water went the wrong way. Her heart was knocking violently inside her chest, but she felt so cold that her lips seemed to have no feeling in them, numb and icy against the glass.

'I couldn't bear it if anything happened to Jamie!'

'I know,' Gabriel said gently, taking away the glass and placing it on the bedside table. He shifted her body so that she lay against him, her head on his shoulder. One hand stroked her hair, offering her an undemanding physical comfort which she accepted with a shiver.

'He's all I've got.'

Gabriel's arm tensed under her shoulder. 'We'll get him back for you,' he promised, his hand continuing to stroke down the soft fall of hair, tidying the strands of it on her shoulder.

'I don't know how I would live if I could never see him again.'

'How do you think I've felt these past two years?' Gabriel broke out huskily. He lifted her chin with one hand and looked into her wide eyes. 'Every morning I've got up and asked myself how I was going to get through yet another day without so much as a glimpse of you. The days have been endless and the nights hell.'

'I'm sorry,' she whispered, her fine dark brows quivering. 'I didn't want to make you unhappy.'

'Unhappy? My God, the word doesn't begin to cover it,' he muttered, his mouth fierce. 'You never gave a damn for me, did you? You couldn't have walked out on me if you had. Why did you marry me if you didn't love me? Was it the money? I didn't think money mattered to you. I'd have sworn on a stack of Bibles that you didn't care twopence about the money. I practically had to force you to accept my presents.'

'Money doesn't make you happy, it often just gets in the way,' Marisa sighed, looking away from him. 'Of course I didn't marry you for the money.'

'Why, then?'

'When I was little we never stayed in one place long enough for me to feel I belonged and everything around me was always changing. I've never been able to feel I belonged anywhere, with anyone, and when you asked me to marry you I knew I wasn't going to feel I belonged with you, either, but I couldn't talk to you about it. You never listened to me.'

'You never said anything,' Gabriel said. 'I asked and asked and you never answered. You just sat there with those great blue eyes fixed on me and never said a damned word.'

'I tried, but I couldn't get the words out. I couldn't believe in you.'

'What do you mean, couldn't believe in me? Couldn't believe I loved you? How could you doubt it? I was ready to give you the moon on a plate. From the minute I first saw you I was obsessed with you, you were never out of my head. I've never stopped thinking about you since the day we met. I wake up in the morning and you're the first thought in my head. I go to bed and you're the last thought I have before I get to sleep. I dream about you. How could you doubt that I really loved you?'

'But will it last?' Marisa cried, her throat hurting with unshed tears.

Gabriel stared at her, his face staggered. 'Will it bloody last? What the hell sort of question is that? You didn't wait around to find out, did you?'

Marisa's whole body stopped with a jerk and then her heart began again at a rapid pace, her lungs continued breathing, her blood went on pumping round her body, while her mind dazedly repeated Gabriel's words over and over again. She hadn't waited to find out. She had fled from her own fear that Gabriel's love wouldn't last, preferring to leave him rather than live in a bitter limbo waiting for his love to stop.

'Do you mean to say that that's why you left me?' Gabriel asked hoarsely. His eyes were flint-like and his features held in a vice of rage. 'You mean to tell me you ran away because you didn't trust me to go on loving you?'

'I couldn't believe it,' Marisa whispered.

'God almighty,' Gabriel muttered, his arm tightening round her. He caught her shoulders and shook her, bending over her furiously. 'You stupid little bitch, are you out of your mind? You couldn't even tell me what was wrong, you couldn't even bring yourself to mention it, but you were prepared to put me through two years of hell just because you'd made up that idiotic mind of yours that I might not go on loving you?'

'I'm sorry.' She was terrified of the violence in his face, the harshness of his voice.

'I could kill you,' Gabriel grated, still shaking her.

White and trembling, she made no effort to free herself, watching him in terror.

For a moment he stared back at her, reading the fear in her face, the whiteness of her skin, the trembling of her lips. His teeth came together and his mouth tightened as he fought for control of his temper. He released her and stood up, turning away.

'It's a great pity you didn't come out with all this two years ago instead of vanishing without a word—but at least it's said now. There's no way I can prove to you that I love you or that I can make you believe I'll go on loving you. I don't think you know the first thing about love. Love involves trust, and your narrow little mind doesn't seem capable of that.' He swung and looked at her again coldly. 'I didn't think I'd ever dislike you, Marisa, but at this moment I find I don't like you very much at all.' Turning away, he strode across the room and slammed out of the door, leaving her silent, staring after him, feeling sick.

CHAPTER FIVE

THERE was some truth in what Gabriel had said
to her about her feelings for him. If he had been
someone she had met in her own world, someone
she worked with, someone she met at a party, she
could have got to know him gradually, dated him
over a longer period, talked to him about herself
and learnt to understand him. She might then
have been able to believe in his love and to feel
brave enough to love him back unreservedly. But
it had all happened too fast and with too much
violence. The immediacy of Gabriel's passion for
her had knocked her off balance and left her too
confused to know what she felt.

The distance between her world and his had
made the whole situation ten times more complic-
ated. How could she believe in his love when the
fairy tale glitter of his background made it impossible?

He had swept her into marriage before she had
had time to think, let alone time to feel. The physical passion between them had had the same
unreality. She had always been too shy to express
her own passion, merely submitting to his with
helpless weakness, while all the time under her
silence she had been resenting her own submis-
sion. The fact that she hid her thoughts, that she

forced down her own emotions, had made it all
build up inside her like a stone wall blanking
Gabriel out of her head and shutting Marisa in
upon herself.

Even now, the problem of her relationship with
Gabriel paled into insignificance beside her anxiety over Jamie. She didn't have time, she
couldn't think, with this fear pressing over her
heart. Her whole attention was consumed by
thoughts of Jamie, all her feelings going out towards her son and leaving no room inside her for
anything else.

Gabriel and the future would have to wait.
Everything would have to wait. Until she had
Jamie back she couldn't spare any part of her
mind or heart for anything but him.

Getting up slowly, her legs weak under her
after the shocks of the last hour, she had a shower
and got dressed. The fitted wardrobe taking up
one whole wall of the bedroom was closely
packed with expensive, beautifully made clothes
which she had scarcely worn and hardly remembered. In the first months of their marriage
Gabriel had enjoyed choosing colours and styles
with her, fascinated by her dazed reaction to the
elegant salon where they had sat watching models
parade to and fro. Looking back, Marisa could
see that Gabriel had got a kick out of showering
her with presents, seeing her incredulous and disbelieving face as he pressed gifts into her hands.

Marisa had never been spoilt in her life. Her
childhood had been narrow and empty. Gabriel,

perhaps, had guessed all that. Perhaps her responses had taught him that much about her, and he had tried to give her the impulsive, immediate pleasures of childhood when he thrust his presents on her. If she had understood him or let him understand her it might have worked.

She took down a dress which she remembered Gabriel choosing. He had always liked to see her wear it, the scooped neckline emphasising her small, high breasts, the flared skirt rustling as she walked. Gabriel liked her in blue. It was his favourite colour.

Dudley tapped on the door and asked if she felt she could eat some breakfast.

'Just coffee, thank you,' Marisa told him.

He went away without comment. She followed him a moment later and found Gabriel in the library, a newspaper spread across his desk, his brooding eyes fixed on the great photograph of Jamie taking up the front page.

He looked up, and she saw his eyes narrow as he took in the dress she was wearing. He remembered it, but he made no comment on her choice, looking back at the newspaper.

'I wouldn't be surprised if the inspector was right. If Jamie had been kidnapped and was in the hands of professional criminals the whole thing would have been handled differently. I think this demand is a phoney.'

Marisa didn't know whether to hope he was right or to pray he was wrong.

'So long as I get him back,' she said drily.

'The trouble with publicity is it always flushes the wrong people out of the forest. They had to make Jamie's face famous, but the nuts are bound to react to all this news coverage.'

'I wish there was something we could do instead of just waiting,' Marisa muttered. 'It's the waiting that's so hard. If you don't know what's happening, what they're doing, you go mad trying to think.'

'Don't try to think. Try to be patient.'

'You don't understand!' Her cry was agonised, but Gabriel looked at her with a muted hostility.

'If I'd had a chance to get to know my own son I might understand a lot better. Instead of that I've only learnt that I have a son when he's vanished.'

Dudley appeared with the coffee. 'Shall I serve it in here, sir?' he asked Gabriel, who looked at Marisa, lifting one brow.

'Please,' she said, sitting down in one of the black leather armchairs.

Dudley placed the tray on a low table beside her and withdrew. Gabriel leaned on the hearth, his grey eyes brooding on her as she poured the coffee.

The telephone rang and Gabriel stiffened. He strode to it; snatched it up. 'Yes?'

Marisa stood up, too, almost knocking over the table, her hands clenched at her sides. Gabriel was listening intently, his face unreadable.

'That's that, then,' he said in heavy tones.

Marisa drew a shaky breath. She could only see

his profile, but he looked grim.

'Well, thank you for letting me know,' said Gabriel. 'Goodbye.'

He replaced the telephone and turned. 'What?' Marisa asked in a barely audible voice, her blue eyes burning on him.

'There was another call to the same newspaper. This time the police were waiting for it and they traced it while the paper kept the man talking. The inspector was right—it was a hoax.'

She limply sat down, her body slack. 'A hoax,' she repeated. 'How cruel, how unbelievably cruel!'

'Probably some lunatic,' Gabriel told her, standing beside her chair but not touching her. 'The inspector advised me that it wouldn't be the last. We might well get some calls like that ourselves.'

'But what are the police doing? Did he say?'

'They're doing everything they can,' Gabriel reassured her. He bent his long body and picked up her cup of coffee, passing it to her. 'Try to relax, for God's sake, Marisa. You're like a bundle of wires.'

'What do you expect? I'm going crazy!'

'With all that publicity there's every hope that someone will remember seeing Jamie. We've got to wait and hope.'

Hope was a stranger to her. She had stopped hoping for anything so long ago she couldn't remember exactly when it had happened. Jamie had made hope seem a possibility. He had brought laughter and life into her dull, quiet world and now it was gone, leaving her worse off than she had been before. She could only look into a dead future.

'I can't just sit here waiting,' she muttered. 'I've got to know.'

'Is that why you left me?' Gabriel asked in a low, bitter voice. 'Because your need to know the worst was so great that you weren't even prepared to give me a chance to prove you were wrong?'

She bent her head, the dark hair falling forward over her shoulder. 'I was a coward.'

'You were,' Gabriel agreed tersely.

'I couldn't understand why you married me.'

'A four-letter word,' Gabriel said. 'Love '

'I didn't believe in it.'

'So I realise now. It wasn't in your dictionary.'

Marisa looked up, thrusting her hair back, her hand trembling. 'You don't believe in something you've never thought you would ever be given.'

His face altered. He drew in his lower lip and watched her with unreadable eyes. 'I realised you weren't close to your parents, but surely when you were a child . . .'

She shook her head. 'They never even knew I existed.'

He frowned and put down his cup, moving away to lean on the back of a chair, his eyes on her. 'So that explains that distant, other-world look of yours. That was what fascinated me from the start. You looked lost and vulnerable, incredibly fragile. I was almost afraid I was imagining you.'

'I sometimes used to think I was imagining myself,' she confessed, a wry faint smile on her mouth. 'Everything around me seemed a long way away as though I saw it all through a window, but I was outside and I didn't think I'd ever get into the room where it was all happening.'

'All happening?' he repeated, frowning.

She shrugged. 'I don't know—life, I suppose.'

Gabriel stared at her fixedly. 'I'm beginning to think that instead of marrying you, I should have taken you to see a psychiatrist!'

She laughed and their eyes met in startled disbelief. It was the first time she could ever remember laughing spontaneously at anything he said to her.

'From what you've said it sounds to me as if you were in a state of deep depression when I met you,' he told her quite gently. 'If I hadn't been so obsessed with my own feelings for you I might have taken the time to look at you closely and realise you weren't . . .' He broke off and Marisa smiled drily.

'Weren't quite right in the head?'

Gabriel grimaced. 'That's putting it a bit dramatically, but I wonder if you weren't in need of treatment of some kind for this depression. Your family background didn't add up to me at the time but I wasn't thinking too clearly myself. I was so desperate to get you married that I thought of very little else. Maybe we were both in the grip of an obsession. I was obsessed with you, but not the real person I'd met—I see that now. I'd dreamed up my own version of you from the way you looked. I didn't stop to ask myself how real my dream girl was—I just grabbed at her.'

'I think I knew that,' Marisa said quietly. 'I got the feeling you didn't really love me at all, you just wanted me, the way you might have seen a doll in a shop window and gone in to buy it.'

He flushed, his mouth hardening. 'That's not very kind.'

'It was the feeling I got from you. You almost forced me to marry you and I couldn't seem to get across to you that I wasn't sure.'

'You got it across,' Gabriel said roughly. 'I knew damned well you didn't feel the way I did, but then you were so young. I thought it was because I was fifteen years older than you. I had a few qualms of conscience about marrying you because of our age gap, but it never occurred to me that there was a hell of a lot more to it than that.'

'Can you imagine what it felt like to me to be brought here after the way I'd always lived?' she demanded. 'If I'd felt lost before, I felt ten times more lost in this house. I didn't know what to do. I felt I'd got trapped in a nightmare. The servants, the parties, the way your friends talked and looked at me with contempt—I was so far out of my depth I was drowning, but I couldn't find a way of telling you.'

Gabriel came slowly back and knelt down

beside her, taking one of her cold white hands between both of his own. 'You're telling me now,' he said softly. 'And I'm listening. Keep talking, darling.'

Marisa looked at him in surprise. 'I am talking, aren't I?' A little colour flowed into her cheeks. 'I can't remember ever saying so much to anyone in my life before.'

'You were the most silent creature I'd ever met,' he told her. 'It didn't matter to me at the beginning. I only wanted to look at you.'

'Do you think I didn't know that? You used to stare and I wondered what you were seeing. I knew it wasn't me.'

Gabriel's dark brows shot upwards. 'Wasn't you?'

'You've said it yourself—you'd invented another me, and that was the wife you thought you had.'

'Was this why you refused to have a baby? I thought you hated the idea of having my child.'

She winced. 'I couldn't be so cruel! No, I was scared about that, too. I kept remembering your first child and I had a horrible feeling that that would happen to my baby if I had one. I thought . . .' She broke off, shivering, and Gabriel watched her with drawn brows.

'You thought you'd lose him?'

She nodded, looking up at him, her pallor returning. 'When I realised Jamie wasn't outside that shop I had the same terrible sinking sensation. I think I'd always expected something to snatch him away from me. Jamie was too good to be true. I'd got used to believing he was mine and that he loved me, but at the back of my head I always wondered when it would happen.'

'My God,' Gabriel muttered in a low voice. 'Marisa! Haven't you ever been happy?'

'With Jamie, yes,' she said. 'Jamie was mine, all mine.'

'He was mine, too,' Gabriel told her, his voice assertive, insisting that she face the fact.

Marisa nodded, her lips dry, moistening them with the tip of her tongue before she felt she could speak. 'I'm sorry.'

'How did you manage? You must have had a bad time, trying to keep a baby on a small salary.'

'Sally helped. She was fantastic. She had so many problems of her own, but she wouldn't let me do half as much as I would have liked to do in return. She and Joe were real friends, and they loved Jamie. I was happy in their house.'

'Tell me about them,' Gabriel asked as if he were really interested, and she hesitantly began to explain about Joe's stroke and Sally's agency, the way she had divided her day between work and looking after Jamie. She sketched in her life for him without realising what she was doing, giving him a clear little picture of the months they had been apart.

'Sally and Joe sound like marvellous people,' Gabriel said when she came to a surprised halt some time later. 'I'm grateful to them for the way they looked after my wife and son.'

She knew he had phrased that deliberately, and she looked at him with hesitance.

'Don't . . .' She stopped after the first word, swallowing.

'Don't what?' Gabriel asked keenly.

She looked away, biting her lip. 'Don't rush me, Gabriel.'

He was silent, staring at her averted face.

'Not this time,' Marisa said huskily. 'All I can think about is Jamie. He's my whole world. Until I've got him back I shan't know.'

'Know what?' Gabriel asked, his voice deep.

'Anything,' Marisa said wryly. 'I feel as though the clocks have stopped and I'm just waiting for life to begin again, or . . .'

'Or?'

'Or not,' she said.

'Don't think like that!' Gabriel blazed, grabbing her chin and wrenching her face round so that he could look into it. 'Hasn't all that we've just said shown you anything? You've run away from life for years. What good has it done you? You've been so busy trying not to get hurt that you've almost destroyed yourself. Stop running, Marisa. Try taking a few risks with life. It may surprise you.'

'I took a risk when I married you,' she pointed out.

'You didn't take it,' Gabriel said. 'I forced it on you. Maybe I shouldn't have done that. I should have taken the time to get to know you properly instead of snatching at you like a desperate man trying to save something from a shipwreck.'

'I always felt I was just another object in this house and one which didn't have much value or much future.' Marisa looked around the library at the banked rows of books, the polished mahogany furniture, the floor-length crimson velvet curtains. 'I was one of your possessions, that's all. I wasn't really needed.'

'You were needed,' Gabriel told her, framing her face between cupped hands and staring into her eyes. 'I needed you too much. I see now that I almost killed you with my need. I was only thinking about myself when I should have thought about you.'

She frowned, her lashes flickering in confusion. 'That applies to me, too, doesn't it? We neither of us understood the other. We both only thought of ourselves.'

He leaned forward and brushed her eyes with a light kiss, closing them, the pale lids quivering under his mouth. 'Maybe that's all people ever do. I was projecting my own desire on to you. I wanted to believe you were the girl I thought I'd met. Whenever something didn't seem to fit I was ready to ignore it or force it to match the picture in my head. I felt I was getting past the age when I might ever meet my dream woman, I suppose, and you fitted loosely. I was determined to make you be what I wanted you to be.'

'Life is too difficult for human beings,' said Marisa, a sigh shivering through her. 'Isn't it? When you can't get through to the other person, when words just don't seem to mean anything, how are we supposed to know what we're doing?'

'Trust,' Gabriel suggested.

Marisa looked at him with dry irony. 'That's something I never learned to do.'

'No, nor me,' he said, surprising her. He caught her start and quick look and gave her a slow smile. 'Hasn't it occurred to you that I haven't had much cause to trust anyone, either? When you know perfectly well that people lie to you and want to get all they can out of you because of your money, you don't trust anyone. One of the reasons I became obsessed with you was because you obviously didn't want my money. You showed no interest in possessions of any kind. You had to be reminded to wear the jewellery I gave you. You never asked me for anything—you looked more harassed than delighted when I gave you anything.'

'I felt you were using your money to trap me.'

'Binding you with hoops of gold?' he asked shrewdly.

She nodded. 'The more you gave me the worse I felt.'

'If only you'd come out with it! We could have saved ourselves two years of misery.' He looked at her through his black lashes in a secretive, brooding way. 'Did you miss me at all?'

Marisa hesitated. She could tell him the truth and see his face darken, or tell him a lie and hate herself. But what was the truth? she wondered. She no longer knew. The great silent gulf between them had closed so far during the past hour that she no longer knew.

'I wouldn't let myself think about you,' she said, compromising. 'And once Jamie was born I never thought about anything but him.' She paused and added softly: 'Except when he reminded me of you despite all my efforts to forget you.'

'I'm beginning to see I owe my son a lot,' Gabriel muttered. 'At least he stopped you from forgetting me altogether.'

'I never really knew you,' Marisa said. Didn't he realise that? They were strangers who had been married and lived in the same house without ever getting to know one another. She had learnt more about him in the last twenty-four hours, and told him more about herself, than they had learnt of each other in the months of their marriage.

'What did you feel about me?' he asked huskily, fingering the delicate modelling of her face, like a blind man feeling his way across her cheek down to the soft curve of her mouth.

She drew back nervously. Gabriel felt the withdrawal and his eyes darkened.

'I hate it when you shrink away from me!'

'I can't help it. I don't mean to do it.'

'What are you afraid I'll do to you? Do you think I want to hurt you?' The gentle, caressing hand had become harsh, closing round her chin and biting into her soft flesh.

She froze, feeling the violence inside him. Gabriel looked at her, his grey eyes probing her face, an icy anger in them.

He dragged her to her feet, his face closed in that cold rage, and his mouth came down in a fierce, searching movement, closing over her lips and parting them. Marisa was too startled to resist in the first moment. Her mouth quivered weakly under the attack of his kiss. Gabriel's hands released her shoulders and began to move over her in a sensuous exploration. A strange melting heat began inside her. She had always felt that she was the victim of Gabriel's physical passion, resenting him even as she gave in to him. She had never felt a returning passion which could match his, but now the hungry coaxing movements of his mouth were awakening the first, tentative response in her.

She put her hands against his chest and felt the muscled flesh beneath that silk shirt lifting and falling in rapid excitement, his heart beating hard and fast. Her head sank back and Gabriel deepened his kiss, one of his hands sliding up to touch her breast in a soft, possessive caress.

Her eyes closed she relinquished her hold on her mind, letting her hands steal up to his neck and close around it. Her lips began moving under his, clinging, returning the pressure of his mouth.

Gabriel lifted his head at last, taking a deep hoarse breath. Marisa opened her eyes, dazed, and he looked down at her with a flushed face.

'That,' he said thickly, 'was real communication.'

Her skin burned. She pushed him away, feeling oddly shaky and weak.

'I must go and . . .' She did not know how to finish that sentence. She had begun it feverishly without thinking it through. Gabriel laughed under his breath and she turned away and almost ran out of the room.

Back in her bedroom she sank down on the bed, clasping her hot face between both hands. What had happened just now? For the first time in Gabriel's arms she had not felt afraid after the first moment. She had no idea what she had felt, only that there had been some sort of feeling moving inside her, like water flowing under ice, silent and out of sight.

She had never allowed herself to feel freely towards Gabriel. She hadn't felt safe enough. Emotion was like a hostage given to fate which she had been sure would be dangerous, disastrous. She had married a myth and never known if the myth existed in real life. The myth had taken on flesh for her today. Talking to Gabriel, listening to Gabriel, feeling the touch of his hands on breast and waist, she had been brought to recognise that he existed and in the same world as herself. He was right: that had been real communication. Their long conversation had pried open the dark door between them and brought them face to face.

She got up and looked at herself in the mirror. A stranger looked back at her, all the remote pallor gone from that face, a deep flush covering her from brow to jaw. Her eyes looked feverish, wildly excited, flickering between their long dark lashes in restless arousal.

Downstairs she heard the shrill of the telephone. After a few rings it cut off and Marisa rushed to the door and ran down the stairs, almost tripping in her haste. Dudley was speaking. He turned and she looked at him in anguished enquiry.

He shook his head, his eyes kind, and said into the receiver: 'I'm sorry, neither of them is available.'

Marisa slumped against the banister. Dudley looked up at her limp figure.

'The press, madam. They keep ringing.'

She nodded, turning to go back upstairs. Gabriel loomed in the door of the library, his black head still dishevelled after their long embrace.

'You must eat something,' he commanded calmly. 'Dudley, get us some lunch right away. Something simple.'

Dudley said: 'My wife's got the meal waiting, sir. We thought chicken.'

'Fine,' said Gabriel, beckoning to Marisa with a long, determined hand. 'We'll have it now.'

She slowly walked towards him and as she did so the telephone began again. Dudley went back to it and she heard him repeat the same ritual. Gabriel gave her a calming smile.

'The minute there's any real news, we'll get it.'

'But when?' she asked. 'When, Gabriel?'

He shrugged, giving her a helpless look. 'Rhetorical questions won't help. It will do Jamie a lot more good if you eat something. Otherwise

you're going to collapse and when he does come
home he won't find you waiting for him.'

Marisa had to see the sense of that. She forced
herself to eat some of the lunch under Gabriel's
insistent eyes and found she was far less reluctant
than she had been. Her body was asserting its
need for food. She was using up energy, both
mental and physical, at a far faster rate than
normal and her appetite surprised her.

After they had sat in silence drinking their
coffee, Gabriel went off to ring the police to check
if there was any shred of news, however small.
When he came back she looked at him pleadingly
and he shook his head without a word.

'Nothing at all?' Her heart turned over and her
hands went cold again. She had somehow convinced herself that there was hope, after all, and
the withdrawal of it made her feel sick.

'Not yet. It is only twenty-four hours, Marisa.'

'Only!'

'I know, it seems like a lifetime. I feel the same
myself. This time yesterday I was working as
normal, never suspecting what was going to hit
me.'

She looked at her hands. 'This time yesterday I
was in the park with Jamie, pushing him on a
swing.' She had a crystal clear picture of it in her
mind—the grey winter sky, the bare trees, the
empty park and Jamie laughing as she pushed
him.

'What a difference one day can make,' Marisa
sighed.

'Yes,' Gabriel agreed, watching her through those thick black lashes, his hard face intent. 'Does Jamie like swings?'

Her smile flashed out, surprising both of them. 'He loves them, but he doesn't like going too high or too fast. He's cautious.'

'Like his mother.'

She smiled again, a faintly teasing look in her eyes. 'He's far braver than I am. If he falls over he won't cry, unless he's really hurt. He gets up with his lip sticking out and looks furious. Usually he blames whatever is nearest. Naughty chair, he says, kicking it. That's more like you.'

'Oh, I go around all day kicking chairs and talking to them,' Gabriel agreed, smiling.

The telephone went. They both tensed, avoiding each other's eyes. Dudley's low voice answered it. They heard his voice rise, then he walked towards the door and Gabriel was on his feet and moving towards it before Dudley opened it.

'What is it?' he asked.

'Someone who says he knows where Master Jamie is, sir,' Dudley stuttered, the words falling over themselves to get out.

Gabriel was out of the door and striding to the phone before Dudley had stammered the last word.

Marisa ran after him, trembling.

'Gabriel Radley speaking,' she heard Gabriel say urgently into the phone.

She could not hear what the person at the other

end was saying, but she stood close beside Gabriel, watching his intent face, trying to guess whether the news was good or bad from his expressions.

'How much?' he demanded suddenly, then: 'Yes, yes, I give you my word. How much?'

There was another silence, then he said: 'Yes.' The burr of the other voice went on for several minutes. Gabriel listened, getting a pen out of his inner jacket pocket and gesturing to Dudley to fetch him the large pad lying nearby. He wrote in a rapid, jerky hand which betrayed his anxiety. Marisa, her whole body shaking with hope and fear, watched.

'Right,' said Gabriel. 'I've got that.'

There was another pause, then he said: 'I understand. Yes, I give you my word. No, the police will not be involved. Of course I believe you. When shall I . . .?'

There was more burring, then he said: 'Very well. I'll be there.'

The phone clicked and he hung up slowly. Marisa asked feverishly: 'Jamie's all right?'

'He's fine, if he was telling the truth, just fine.'

'What was he saying? He was the man who kidnapped Jamie?'

'No,' said Gabriel.

The telephone shrilled again and Gabriel picked it up. 'Hallo, Inspector,' he said calmly. 'You heard?'

Marisa felt a dart of agony. He had promised the police wouldn't be involved, and he couldn't break his word. They might never see Jamie again. She put a hand over Gabriel's arm, shaking him, her face white.

'You can't risk Jamie's life. You promised!'

Gabriel gave her a brief glance. 'Hold on a moment, Inspector.' He covered the mouth of the receiver and turned towards her. 'Jamie isn't going to be at risk for one second.'

'How can you be sure of that?'

'I am sure,' Gabriel said firmly.

'If anything happens because you didn't keep your word I'll never forgive you,' she whispered bitterly.

His eyes hardened. 'Can't you start trusting me even now, Marisa?' There was contempt in the look he gave her as he turned back to the phone. 'Hallo, Inspector. Sorry about that. Yes, I agree, that's the way we'll play it.'

Marisa swayed against the wall, her face ice cold. Gabriel was going to co-operate with the police, even if it meant risking Jamie's life.

CHAPTER SIX

WHEN he had hung up, Gabriel turned and looked at Dudley. 'Tell them to get my car round.'

'Yes, sir,' said Dudley, not moving.

Gabriel lifted one brow. 'What is it?'

'Good luck, sir,' Dudley said on a muttered note of embarrassment before hurrying away, his usually stolid face flushed, as though he felt horrified at having stepped out of his usual role.

'What are you going to do?' Marisa asked in a dry little voice as Gabriel glanced at her.

'I'm going to find my son,' Gabriel told her curtly. He looked at his watch. 'I want you to stay here.'

'No!' she flared, her eyes defying him.

'Marisa, don't make me angry with you—not now. I'm not absolutely certain what I'm going to find and I don't want you involved in case it means either trouble or a disappointment.'

'I want to come—I have a right to know,' she insisted.

'We don't know yet whether this time it's genuine.'

'But if it is . . .'

'If it is, it would still be better for you to wait here calmly and sensibly. Believe me, you'd only get in the way, and you'd probably find it very upsetting, if what I was told is true.'

'What did the man say?'

'He claims he lives in the same house as a woman who's suddenly produced a little boy who's the spitting image of Jamie. If it is Jamie he's being well looked after, anyway. This man says he's seen him and Jamie is fine.'

'You were talking about money, though,' Marisa accused, her body tense. 'I heard you. How much? you said.'

'There was a price tag attached to the address where Jamie lives,' Gabriel said drily. 'My informant obviously saw a chance of some easy money. He says he had nothing to do with the abduction of Jamie. He was merely giving me the information, but he wanted to be paid for it.'

'Oh, God,' Marisa muttered, closing her eyes, a tide of sickness rising inside her. 'How can they?'

'You may well ask,' Gabriel drawled. 'The police were tapping the line, of course. The man clearly didn't expect that. But I did give him my word, and there's a reward offered for information leading to the discovery of Jamie, so he's committed no crime. The police won't move against him. The Inspector's men will watch from a safe distance until I give the signal, then they will move in once we're sure that the man who rang is genuine and that Jamie really is at this address.'

'Let me come,' Marisa begged, clasping his arm with both hands and looking at him with pleading eyes. 'I want to be with him.'

'Marisa, you aren't thinking straight. There could be a very unpleasant scene with this woman. She's got to be sick, probably mentally unbalanced, distraught. When the police arrive God knows what sort of scene there'll be.'

'Jamie,' Marisa whispered, shuddering.

'He won't get hurt, they'll make sure of that. Neither will this woman—but she might very well cry and scream before they get her out of the house, and you wouldn't enjoy that, would you?'

'Jamie will be upset,' she protested.

'There'll be a policewoman there. And a doctor. Jamie will be fine.'

Marisa looked at him uncertainly and Gabriel touched her cheek with one hand. 'Please, Marisa, just do as I ask, and wait here. You'll have Jamie back safely if anything I can do can bring it about.'

Dudley came back and Gabriel turned to him. 'Look after Mrs Radley while I'm gone.'

'Yes, sir,' said Dudley, moving close to her as though ready for any contingency.

Gabriel moved to the door, shrugging into the heavy dark overcoat which Dudley had been carrying.

'The press are still outside, sir,' Dudley told him.

'I might drive over a few,' said Gabriel with grim humour as he opened the door. He gave Marisa a brief look before he closed it. She listened to the engine note. The car roared away towards the gates.

'Can I get you anything, madam?' Dudley

asked, hovering around her anxiously.

She shook her head, moving back into the draw-ing-room. The small gold lyre clock chimed softly in the room. It was late afternoon again. The darkness had fallen. Dudley drew the cur-tains, shutting out the cold winter gloom, and the soft flowering of the standard lamp gave the room a new warmth.

'Are you sure you wouldn't like some tea, madam?' Dudley asked, watching her as she rest-lessly moved around the room.

She looked at him blankly. 'Oh, yes, yes, please.' It would be some occupation, something to keep her mind off what was happening.

Dudley looked around like someone searching for a toy to keep a bored child happy. 'Would you like to watch the television, madam?'

She almost laughed, then she nodded, sinking into one of the deep brocade-upholstered arm-chairs.

Dudley went over to the cabinet which housed the television set and opened the doors. 'Which side, madam?'

'I don't care,' she said, half irritated.

He switched the set on and stood back. 'I'll get you your tea, madam.'

She nodded as he went to the door, her eyes watching the picture come swooping out of no-where. It was children's television. A round black spider was dangling up and down on a piece of wire, a squeaky voice issuing from it. Marisa watched without really listening. The moving wallpaper kept her eye engaged without touching her mind.

When Dudley came back the soft movements disturbed her and she looked round, the little jerk she gave betraying her nervous state.

He placed the tea tray, bending towards her. 'Mrs Dudley thought you might care for some cake, madam.'

Marisa looked at the heavy fruit cake with distaste which she managed somehow to conceal. 'How kind! It looks very good.'

'Her fruit cake is excellent,' Dudley agreed, pouring the tea. 'She wondered if Master Jamie had any favourite foods, madam, that she could make, just in case.'

Marisa swallowed. 'He likes most food, but only if it's quite simple. He doesn't like highly spiced food.'

'No, children don't, do they?'

'He doesn't like vegetables much, either. A few peas and sometimes carrots, but never spinach or cabbage.'

'Does he like sponge cake, madam? Mrs Dudley makes a very good jam sponge.'

'Jamie loves jam sponge.'

Dudley looked pleased, standing back in an erect position, obviously fully intending to stay on duty, watching over her as Gabriel had asked him to do.

Marisa broke off a piece of the fruit cake and put it into her mouth. It tasted like sawdust. She chewed, wondering how to persuade Dudley to go away without sounding rude.

Providentially the telephone rang. Dudley departed reluctantly, and Marisa heard him telling the caller that nobody was at home. When he came back she had secreted a large piece of the fruit cake behind her cushion. Dudley looked at the plate with satisfaction.

'Another piece of cake, madam?' His hand hovered over the cake knife and Marisa hurriedly shook her head.

'I couldn't, it was very good, but I'm not really hungry.'

'More tea, madam?'

'Thank you,' she said despairingly.

'Mrs Dudley was wondering which room you intended to give Master Jamie, madam.'

'Room?' Marisa tried to drag her mind round to this problem, her brows wrinkling. 'Oh, I think we could think of that later.'

'He would be needing a cot, madam,' Dudley pointed out.

'His is at our flat,' said Marisa, realising that she had not yet considered the future. She had been too absorbed in the anxiety over Jamie himself to realise that things would never be the same again for them.

She did not need to think twice about what Gabriel's plans would be. He was not going to let her take his son out of this house. And did she want to, anyway?

She pushed that away, biting her lip. All that was something to think about when all this was safely over. For the moment all that mattered was to get Jamie back.

'Where would he sleep tonight, madam?' Dudley asked.

'With me,' Marisa said decisively.

Dudley's brows indicated shock. 'Of course, madam,' he said blandly.

Marisa had had enough of his company. She wanted to be alone, to wait with all the patience she could muster, all her attention given to Jamie.

'I think I'll try to sleep,' she lied. 'Could you turn off the television, Dudley?'

'Of course, madam, very wise,' he said, almost with the same relief she felt, going over to switch off the set. She lay down with her head resting on the cushion, and Dudley tiptoed to the door as though she was already asleep, leaving the soft glow of the lamp spreading a circle of light on the other side of the room, but turning off all the other lights. He closed the door and the room sank into blissful silence. Marisa lay staring at the light, her eyes heavy. She had slept very little last night. Her body was aching with exhaustion and she felt herself sinking into a sort of waking stupor. The lyre clock chimed and she jerked out of it, her nerves leaping. She looked at the clock. Gabriel had been gone for an hour, she realised in shock.

What was he doing? Why wasn't he back yet? She swung her legs off the sofa, dislodging the cushion, and looked with distaste at the very squashed piece of cake which had been lying under it.

How was she to get rid of that? Carefully she swept it into her palm and went out of the room, concealing her hand against her side in case Dudley was lurking about in the hall.

She flushed away the cake in her bathroom, washed and renewed her make-up in some sort of effort to make herself feel normal. When she went back downstairs, Dudley was in the hall, trying to look like part of the furniture.

'Can I get you anything, madam?' he asked, floating forward as she got to the foot of the stairs.

'What is the right time, please?'

'Six o'clock, madam,' Dudley told her. 'Would you like a cocktail? A sherry?'

'A cocktail, please,' she said. Anything to make him go away and leave her alone.

He asked what she would like, presenting her with yet another problem that involved her thinking instead of sitting down to brood over Jamie. She looked at him wryly. He meant well. No doubt he told himself that it was best for her not to sit around thinking, worrying, unable to breathe properly because of the fear crushing her lungs and making her feel sick. Maybe he was right. At this precise moment she was only able to think what pleasure it would give her to pelt him with some of the sofa cushions until he left her alone.

He withdrew, taking the tea tray with him, and came back all too soon with her cocktail in a silver shaker. He made a great business of pouring it for her, watching her sip it with the concerned face of an artist waiting for appreciation of a masterpiece.

The sound of a car made her hand shake, and the icy liquid leapt over the side of the glass as it tilted, sprinkling her skirt. Dudley murmured, clicking his tongue. Marisa pushed him away when he tried to dab at her skirt. She was on her feet and out of the room before the car engine had cut out.

Flinging open the door, she looked into the darkness, the light streaming behind her. Her terrified eyes focused on the car and the emerging figure. The chauffeur was hurrying round to hold the door open, but Gabriel had already straightened, turning.

Marisa's heart stopped. 'Jamie!'

She flew down the steps, sobbing, tears streaming down her face. Gabriel put the small, swaddled figure into her open arms and she held Jamie tightly, covering the top of his head with kisses, her body shaking with sobs.

Gabriel put an arm around her, urging her back up the steps into the house. Flashes exploded behind them somewhere in a mimic artillery. Marisa barely noticed them, but Gabriel pushed her back into the house and slammed the front door.

'Bloody cameramen,' he said to Dudley. 'They were trying to climb all over the car as we came through the gates.'

Marisa had unwrapped Jamie from the large tartan blanket swathing him. His sleepy, puzzled, flushed face stared at her. He was in warm blue winceyette pyjamas and tiny blue fur bedroom slippers which had a teddy bear motif on the front of them.

'Mumma,' he said, recognising her with a drowsy smile.

She tried to smile back, her lips quivering, but she couldn't quite make it. The hot tears running down her face wouldn't stop, although she tried to halt them, brushing a hand across her eyes.

She told herself that she mustn't upset Jamie. He mustn't be worried by seeing her cry. Stop it! she scolded herself. She had barely shed a tear while Jamie was missing, but now the tears seemed to be coming out of her like Niagara Falls. She felt as though she was crying for far more than Jamie's safe return to her.

'Bed for this young man, I think,' Gabriel said beside her. 'Will you let me carry him upstairs?'

Marisa shook her head, her arms tightening around Jamie. Not for anything would she relinquish him to anyone else tonight.

'He was asleep in a cot,' Gabriel said very quietly. 'He's very tired.'

Jamie yawned, his face splitting open in that unguarded childish way. Watching him, Marisa started to laugh through her tears, and over her bent dark head Gabriel and Dudley looked at each other. In the doorway behind them Mrs Dudley stood staring, her plump hands clasped in a strangling grip.

Marisa went up the stairs and laid Jamie in her own bed. Eyes screwed shut, he turned on to his face, humping himself into his favourite position.

Marisa stood beside the bed, listening. It was the most beautiful sound she had ever heard. She could stand there all night listening to the soft snuffling Jamie made when he was asleep. Gabriel touched her arm, gesturing to the door, but she shook her head. No way was she leaving this room.

Gabriel's mouth was wry. 'He'll be fine. He's fast asleep and perfectly happy.'

'I'll stay for a while, all the same.'

'You can't watch him twenty-four hours a day without making him feel as nervous as you are,' Gabriel said.

'He might fall out of the bed.' She had arranged pillows in a bank on either side of him, but she still felt worried about him rolling over and falling out.

'Then we'll get Mrs Dudley to sit with him for a while,' Gabriel told her. 'She'd be delighted.' He went out and Marisa sat down on the edge of the bed, watching the small hump breathing, the tousled brown curls buried half under the sheet. Jamie's hand was curled beside his face, and she bent over and touched it lightly with one finger. He didn't stir. Jamie slept like a log. While she had been half out of her mind with terror, he had probably been a little puzzled by his strange surroundings, the unfamiliar face, but she did not think he had been through any traumatic shock. If he had, it would have showed. It had all been a

strange adventure to him; in a few days he would
have forgotten all about it. She knew she never
would.

Gabriel returned with Mrs Dudley panting at
his heels. She gave Marisa a tearful smile. It surprised Marisa to see the damp eyes. She had not
even set eyes on the woman during the last
twenty-four hours, yet she was crying with the
same relief Marisa was feeling.

'Oh, I'm so glad,' Mrs Dudley whispered,
giving a quick look at the bed. 'He's well away,
isn't he? I'll stay with him. He'll be safe with
me.'

'Thank you,' said Marisa, a prickly feeling
inside her. It was ridiculous to feel a sort of resentment. Mrs Dudley was being very kind, but
Marisa did not really want to leave Jamie in her
care. She didn't ever want to leave Jamie alone
again for one second. She hesitated, and Gabriel
took her arm in a determined grip and steered her
towards the door.

Outside on the landing she gave him a stifled
stare of anger. He had forced her to abandon her
son to a stranger again.

'I'd rather stay,' she said in a low voice.

'I realise that, but you're very hyper tonight—
you need to wind down before you go right
through the top of your head.'

'I'm fine.' She rubbed a hand across her wet
face. The tears had stopped and she felt very
shaky, her legs not quite steady as she let Gabriel
guide her down the stairs.

'What we both need is a drink,' he told her, moving to the table on which stood crystal decanters. He poured whisky for himself, brandy for her.

'I don't want it,' she said sulkily, not taking the glass.

'You need it,' he told her, winding her fingers firmly around the glass. He lifted it to her mouth. 'Take a sip.'

She swallowed, shuddering. 'Vile!'

'You'll get used to the taste.' He stood in front of her, his own glass in his hand, staring into the amber liquid for a moment before he raised it to his lips and swallowed some of the whisky. Marisa wondered what he was thinking about; his hard, sardonic face gave her no clue.

The brandy circulated in her veins, lending her a heat she had not had, relaxing her muscles from the tension which had held them.

'What happened?' she asked quietly.

Gabriel looked into his glass, his mouth twisting. 'Nothing very much. It was all very quick, very discreet. I met the man outside a local pub, as arranged. He was telling the truth. I gave him some money, he gave me the address. The police moved in—they'd followed me and were watching from across the road.'

'You promised him!'

'He won't get into any trouble. He might hear a few home truths from the Inspector, but there'll be no charges.'

'And the woman?' Marisa asked in a shivering

voice. 'What sort of woman was she?'

Gabriel glanced at her, lifted his glass to his lips and finished the whisky in one swallow. 'Rather a pathetic woman. I felt sorry for her. Apparently she had a little boy the same age as Jamie, but he died last year, and her husband went off with another woman a month ago.'

'Oh, no!' Marisa muttered. She had wondered what sort of woman could steal her child, but she had not had any clear idea of the reasons anyone would have for doing such a thing.

'She was going quietly out of her mind, I guess,' Gabriel said. He moved to the decanter and poured himself another drink. Marisa watched him, wondering if he was far more disturbed than he was letting her see.

Marisa was thinking, her brow furrowed. 'The pyjamas, the slippers—were they . . .?'

'Her little boy's,' Gabriel said curtly.

'Oh.' Marisa closed her eyes. 'Poor woman!' She had Jamie safely back; she could afford to feel pity. What must that woman have been going through? 'What will happen to her?'

'Nothing,' Gabriel said in a deep voice. 'A little psychiatric help, that's all. She's sick—she needs help, not punishment. She snatched Jamie on a moment's impulse. She saw him outside the shop, she said. He was crying and she didn't know what came over her, she said.' His voice had an angry sound. 'Poor bitch,' he muttered. 'I felt sick myself.'

'The police weren't . . .'

'Tough with her? No,' he said, lifting his black head to look at her. 'There was a doctor and a policewoman there. They took her away in an ambulance. The doctor had a quick look at Jamie—we didn't want to disturb him more than we could help. Jamie's fine.'

'Yes,' Marisa murmured. 'He looks exactly the same.' She felt as though she had been through a mangle, but Jamie looked just the way he always looked. From a baby's eye point of view the incidents of the past twenty-four hours might seem a little odd, puzzling, faintly worrying, but he could have no conception of the terrible anxieties that had been making her life living hell.

'It's the rest of us who have really felt it,' Gabriel muttered, putting down his glass with a little clink. 'Jamie probably hardly thought about it at all. Life's pretty weird anyway when you're not quite two. Anything can happen. What's been sending us round the bend has passed right over his head.'

'I hope so,' Marisa agreed. Her body was beginning to feel warm and heavy; the brandy had done its work. She lay back with her head against the sofa cushions, closing her eyes. I'm so tired, she thought. I don't think I've ever been so tired in my life. I could sleep for a hundred years, like the princess who pricked her finger, but I mustn't sleep yet. I must go back upstairs to Jamie. Her arm slackened and fell against her body.

Gabriel stood watching her then bent and picked her up, her head drooping down against his arm. He carried her up the stairs.

CHAPTER SEVEN

OVER the next few days the disturbed rhythm of Marisa's mind slowly began to return to normal. Jamie's presence made it easier. With the carefree acceptance of childhood, he adapted to his new surroundings so soon that she found his casual cheerfulness contagious. Jamie found nothing particularly strange in living in a big house instead of in a tiny flat over a garage. He woke up, played, ate his meals and went to bed without seeming in the least surprised that everything around him was quite different.

Gabriel had had his cot and all his toys and clothes brought over to the house. Marisa had not gone with him, but she had spoken to Sally on the telephone. It had hurt her that Sally's tone was more guarded than friendly. It had obviously been a blinding shock to Sally to discover the truth about Marisa's past. Talking to her, Marisa picked up some unspoken hint that Sally had always believed Jamie to be illegitimate. Marisa's story of a husband from whom she had run away had not genuinely been believed. It made Sally's kindness and generosity the more admirable, particularly as Sally had never before so much as hinted at the idea.

Bewilderment, curiosity and withdrawal all came over to her in Sally's wary voice.

Marisa had not made any plans for the future; all her mind had been devoted to getting Jamie back. Talking to Sally, she realised, though, that she could not go back there. All that part of her life was over. Sally would merely have been embarrassed if Marisa had suggested coming back. Gabriel Radley was too far removed from the little house in the busy London suburb. Sally could not adapt with Jamie's casual acceptance. Marisa had been whisked out of Sally's world and there was no way back.

'I'm sorry, Sally,' she said when they both fell silent, the unspoken things between them choking off their conversation.

Sally didn't pretend not to understand. 'Forget it, love,' she said gruffly. 'It was nice having you and Jamie. Both Joe and I hope you'll make it this time.' She paused and added: 'I liked him—your husband. He seemed a nice man.'

Marisa flushed. She did not want to talk about Gabriel. Perhaps Sally picked that up, too, because she changed the subject and shortly afterwards they said goodbye. Marisa put down the phone, feeling melancholy. The end of something is always sad even when it may be the beginning of something better. Human nature has a dislike of finality.

That night she dreamt that she was in a railway station waiting-room. The dark oak panelling, the stone floor, had a Victorian feel to them. Outside she could hear the whistle of trains, the rattling of wheels, but she was not listening to them. She was waiting, although she did not know what she was waiting for, her body tense with a fevered expectancy. She stared at the doorway. Any moment someone would come through it. Marisa did not know who she was waiting for—no name, no face accompanied that febrile excitement. It was not by any particular incident that the dream remained with her when she woke up. It was the peculiar, deep intensity of her own emotions which stayed with her.

Her flight from emotion had left her suspended in cold space for years. The memory of her own feelings during that dream haunted her.

What had the dream meant? She puzzled over it during the day. Dreams were usually dramatic things if one remembered them. She could remember dreams full of terrifying threat, but she had always been able to trace them back to some fear inside herself or to some symbol which carried its own meaning. People shared dreams. At some time in a life most people dream of falling, flying, snakes or grim pursuit; Marisa knew enough about dreams to know that. The unconscious presents us with cloudy parables which can unravel some problem for us if we understand them. We tell ourselves stories while we sleep, coming to terms with our worries or assessing what has happened to us while we were awake.

But what did it mean to dream about waiting in a railway station for someone we never name? What significance did a railway station have, for heaven's sake?

A place where one started a journey, she thought. Or ended one. Did it matter which? Was it the journey that mattered? Was her mind merely pointing out to her that she had come to a break point in her life?

The trouble with the method the unconscious chose to use in communicating with the conscious mind was that those cloudy parables were far from simple to decipher.

Gabriel wasn't much in evidence during that first week. The day following Jamie's return there was a flurry of activity on the stock exchange and Gabriel vanished from sight for most of the daylight hours, dealing with a constantly changing financial situation. Marisa knew little of it. Gabriel gave her crisp explanations that went right over her head. All she understood was that Gabriel wasn't around, and she was grateful for that. She felt the last thing she could cope with was Gabriel. He was a problem she was pushing to one side while she dragged herself back to some sort of normality.

It was the week before Christmas. The elegant house underwent a sudden transformation when Dudley, his wife and Marisa decorated a large Christmas tree and put up glittering decorations around the ground floor rooms. Jamie sat on the floor, his pink feet bare, pulling a multi-coloured paper chain to pieces in a concentrated, thoughtful way. He approved of the decorations, although his main interest was in trying to eat some of them.

'Not in your mouth, darling,' Marisa told him, detaching a large red foil star from him.

'Time for his tea,' said Mrs Dudley, looking at the clock. 'Would you like me to take him down to the kitchen, Mrs Radley? Give you a break.'

Marisa opened her mouth to refuse when she caught Mrs Dudley's eye and smiled. 'Thank you.'

Jamie was carried off in triumph, poking one pink finger into Mrs Dudley's ear. Marisa had been keeping him almost entirely to herself during the past week. She had needed to see him every time she looked up. But it hadn't escaped her that Mrs Dudley was itching to get him to herself. What was it about babies, puppies, kittens, that fascinated people so much? It wasn't just that they made women feel maternal, protective—it was partly that playing with them gave adults a chance to renew their own childhood, put them in touch with feelings and enjoyments they had forgotten. Even Dudley could be seen hanging around Jamie in his pushchair making funny faces at him, although if caught he would move away with a pink face and a hurriedly re-arranged expression.

Marisa had been wearing jeans and a sweater while she did the Christmas tree. Looking at her watch, she decided she should go up and change. Jamie was late having his tea. The ritual of the day had been broken by the Christmas decorations and they were nearly an hour late. Usually by now Jamie was in his bath ducking his submarine with one toe while Marisa tried to wash his back.

She was at the foot of the stairs when she heard the car. Pausing, she watched the door open. Gabriel's tall figure strolled through it. The winter wind tossed his black hair into ruffled disorder and he ran a hand through it, staring at her.

'Hallo, Jamie having his bath now?'

'He's in the kitchen having his tea.' She felt selfconscious, aware of the way he was eyeing her slender figure in the rather shabby jeans. They had seen very little of each other all that week.

'I'm in time for the ceremony, then,' he said, tossing a briefcase on to the polished table, stripping off his overcoat and chucking that after it. 'I hoped I might be.'

'You're early. Is the crisis over?'

'Blew away,' he said drily. 'The market is tottering back to normal. Which gives me time to get acquainted with my son at last.'

'Mrs Dudley is looking after him.' Marisa hesitated, wondering whether to go upstairs and change or whether to stand here like an idiot not knowing what to say to this stranger who was her husband.

'Time for us to have a drink, then,' he murmured, waving her towards the drawing-room.

She sat down reluctantly, her hands on her knees, demurely considering her feet in the small black shoes. What did you talk about when almost any subject was likely to get you into difficult country?

'Do you think we're going to get that snow, after all? It's colder today.' Oh, fabulous, she thought. The weather. Aren't I original?

Gabriel walked round to hand her the glass of sherry. 'Do you want my considered opinion or shall I just answer that off the top of my head?' he asked gravely.

Her cheeks grew pink, as she sipped the sherry. Her eye fell on the Christmas tree. 'How do you like our decorations?' she asked brightly.

Gabriel swivelled and looked at them. 'That fairy looks a bit unsure of herself.' He walked over and adjusted her, his long arm reaching the top of the tree without effort. 'How's that?'

'Fine,' said Marisa.

'How did Jamie like them?' Gabriel inspected the holly and the swags of chains, his glass in his hand, his long body relaxed.

'Very much.' She drank some more of her sherry, wishing she liked it and wondering why it always tasted like cough medicine to her. Some people swore by the stuff—but then tastes differ.

'What are we going to do about him?' Gabriel asked, wandering over to sit down next to her.

She tried not to jerk away or stiffen. Concentrating on her sherry, she asked: 'How do you mean?'

'Shouldn't he have a nurse?'

'No!' Marisa said indignantly, her head coming up. 'I want to look after him myself.'

'Ah,' said Gabriel, his tone unrevealing. 'What about when you want to go out?'

'I'll take him with me.'

'To a party?' Gabriel mocked. 'There are going to be occasions when Jamie wouldn't be exactly welcome.' He caught her eye and held up one hand. 'Don't tell me. Who loves me, loves my child? But you were ready to leave him with a baby-minder before, weren't you?'

'She wasn't a baby-minder, she was a neighbour, and it was only for a few hours every day.'

'The principle's the same. I think you need some help with him. I'll leave it to you to arrange the details, but you must have someone.'

Marisa looked down, shrugging. She did not want to have a full-time nurse in a starched nanny's uniform bustling about organising Jamie's world and trying to exclude her. She had seen them. There would be a tug of war between her and any nanny who tried to steal Jamie's affections from her.

'What about all the invitations?' Gabriel asked, finishing his drink and putting down the glass. He leaned back, his arms folded behind his head, and watched her.

'What invitations?'

'I've had dozens,' he said. 'Christmas parties, New Year parties, God knows what. I haven't had a chance to decide which to accept. I've been too busy.'

Marisa looked aghast. 'I don't want to go to any parties!' She had hated them, the elegant, lifeless events Gabriel had dragged her to during their months together. His friends were polite, scornful, disbelieving. Their arrival together always seemed the signal for exchanged smiles and raised eyebrows. She wasn't going through that again. She hadn't mentioned it during that year because she hadn't been speaking to him at all, but she wasn't putting up with that again. 'I'm not going to any of them,' she added, in case he misunderstood.

His dark brows lifted sardonically. 'Sight unseen?'

'Yes,' she said, obstinacy in every line of her.

'Case dismissed? You're not even going to discuss which of them you might enjoy?'

'I wouldn't enjoy any of them,' she said, with certainty.

'Why not? How do you know?'

'All your friends are stuffy, condescending and boring.'

He whistled under his breath. 'A very blanket condemnation! What have they done to you?'

'Ignored me, sneered at me, talked about me behind my back.' She tried to think of some examples, but they all blurred into one event of grey tedium. 'Do you think I didn't know what they all thought? They made sure I did. Women can say a lot without uttering a syllable. I wasn't left in any doubt that I was a fish out of water and that you were pitied because you'd married me on impulse and were bound to regret it.' A flash of memory came back and her colour burnt. 'I remember one woman who actually said, openly, in front of me, that the alimony would be good, anyway.'

Gabriel laughed, and she looked at him in sheer disbelief.

'It wasn't funny!'

'I think it's hilarious,' Gabriel drawled. 'Can't you see? That's all she would have been thinking of—she was envying you, admiring you for your smart move in grabbing me.'

'Oh, I'm very smart,' Marisa said bitterly. 'They could see that. One look and they all knew I was a nobody.'

Gabriel's mouth hardened. 'Don't be absurd!'

She sat upright, her cheeks hot, her eyes angry. 'Well, look at me! What would any of them think if they walked in here now and saw me in my old jeans with my hair tied back with a piece of ribbon?'

'That depends,' Gabriel said drily.

She looked at him, not sure what his tone meant.

'On the sex of this unknown visitor,' Gabriel mocked. 'If it was female—you may be right. If it was male . . .' He ran his glance over her and smiled. 'If he had eyes in his head he would be thinking what I'm thinking.'

Marisa shot to her feet, her heart missing a beat. 'I'd better go and change,' she stammered.

'That's one habit you're going to have to break,' Gabriel mused as she rushed towards the door. 'I'll cure you of running away if it kills me.'

He came up to the bathroom later when Jamie was already in his bath, thrashing the water with one hand, regardless of Marisa's protests. Gabriel was in his shirt sleeves. Rolling them up, he squatted down beside the bath and began to play with the submarine. Jamie eyed him doubtfully. He wasn't sure yet what he thought of this very tall stranger who could toss him to his shoulder without an effort. Now Gabriel was on Jamie's eye level and not quite so menacing. Jamie reached out and grabbed the submarine back, clutching it to his wet body, glaring at Gabriel.

'He's possessive about his toys,' said Marisa, laughing. A few foam bubbles clung to her cheek where Jamie had patted her.

'Who isn't?' Gabriel drawled, glancing at her obliquely and watching the pink stain run up her face with open amusement.

She pretended not to get the double meaning. Bending, she lifted Jamie out and began to dry him. He watched Gabriel suspiciously. Marisa sprinkled Jamie with talcum and buttoned him into his pyjamas, then Gabriel picked him up and smiled into his lowering little face.

'We're going to have to get to know one another.'

Jamie didn't look too keen. He stared into his father's face, then deliberately put a finger in his eye.

Removing it, Gabriel said: 'Why do I get the feeling he doesn't like me?'

'He explores people's eyes and ears all the time,' Marisa told him, a little defensively.

'You little monster,' Gabriel told Jamie. 'You look as if butter wouldn't melt in your mouth, too.'

He carried Jamie into the small room beside Marisa's which had been turned into a nursery. Jamie cuddled down in the cot, his teddy tucked in beside him. Marisa bent to kiss him and moved to the door. Gabriel stood looking down at his son, his face unreadable, then he followed her.

Gabriel glanced down at her, his grey eyes casually friendly. 'He's making quite a difference to this house already. Mrs Dudley talks of nothing else.'

She wondered if the disturbance in his orderly house bothered him. It didn't seem to. He was more relaxed than she could remember ever seeing him, his powerful face smoothed out in a smile, his manner easy. When Gabriel chose to smile it altered his whole appearance. The strong, arrogant face could acquire charm, the deep voice sound quite gentle.

Over dinner that evening she suddenly remembered how it had felt when she first went out to dinner with him, the odd selfconscious fixity with which they had talked, not aware of anyone around them, all their attention given to each other.

She looked up, a small red spot burning in each cheek, and Gabriel caught her eyes. His face tautened, a muscle jerking beside his mouth. Marisa hurriedly looked away. Surely he couldn't have noticed anything in her face that could give him a clue what she was thinking?

What was she thinking? Why on earth had the memory of that evening flashed back into her

mind and why did she have to betray some of her
feelings to Gabriel like that?

She wasn't mentally ready to face up to any
decisions about her marriage. She wanted time to
think. Gabriel had only come back into her life so
recently after two years' absence. Last time he
had rushed her into a marriage which had ended
in disaster because she wasn't capable of under-
standing him or knowing anything about herself.
She didn't want to repeat that whole bitter pattern. This time she was going to make a carefully
thought out decision in her own time.

'What had you planned for Christmas if parties
are out?' Gabriel asked her over their coffee.

'I hadn't planned anything.' She hadn't even
thought about it until today. 'Jamie and I had a
very quiet Christmas last year.' It had been the
most wonderful Christmas of her whole life. She
had spent most of it alone with Jamie, joining
Sally and Joe for Christmas dinner and present-
giving round a small Christmas tree. Jamie's
presence had made it a very happy period for
them all. He had not understood what was going
on, but he had enjoyed the coloured lights, the
bright paper, the shared laughter.

'Jamie and you,' Gabriel muttered, his mouth
hard.

She looked at him in surprise at the curt tone.
'Yes.'

'Do you know how often you say that? How
long is it going to take you to recognise that I
belong to this family circle, too?' The harsh bite

of his voice revealed something she had not recognised before and which surprised her into
staring at him incredulously. 'You're not shutting
me out again, Marisa. Jamie is *our* son. He isn't
your exclusive property.' He paused and added:
'Nor are you his.'

Was he jealous of Jamie? Or of their mutual
affection? Did he feel that it excluded him?

Gabriel got up from the table and she hesitantly joined him in the drawing-room. He had
switched on a tape of quiet music and was light-
ing a cigar, his eyes fixed on the tip of it. As she
sat down on the sofa he flicked his eyes sideways
to observe her, a sparkle of mockery in his stare.

'That dress looks better on you now than it
did. Or aren't I supposed to notice that you've
put on a little weight? You were as skinny as a
rake when I first met you.'

'I gained a few pounds when I had Jamie,' she
agreed, smoothing down her full skirt selfconsciously.

'That's not all you gained,' he murmured, sitting down beside her, his long body relaxing with
a sigh. 'It's been a hectic week. Let's hope the
market stays quiet for Christmas.'

Conversation between them was still difficult,
especially with this constant flicker of awareness
beating between them. Gabriel shifted, his thigh
touching her, and her breathing was stilled for a
second before it quickened again. Gabriel looked
at her under his lashes and slid an arm along the
back of the sofa behind her head.

'Isn't it time we started to get to know each other? It seems absurd that we've been married three years without knowing the first thing about what makes each other tick.'

'You know more or less everything about me now,' said Marisa, wishing he wouldn't keep moving his eyes over her, a sparkle of mockery behind his smile. She wasn't ready to rush into anything yet. 'Don't rush me,' she added.

'Who's rushing?' She felt his long fingers begin to play with the loose strands of black hair lying across her shoulders. 'I like your hair untied. When you tie it back you look about sixteen.'

'It keeps it out of my eyes.'

'Very practical,' he agreed, smiling sideways at her. The force of his profile betrayed the nature behind it, the driving energy of a man who has always had what he wanted and taken what he had the whim to take. 'Talk to me, Marisa. You've found your tongue at last. Use it.'

'I've told you everything there is to know.' She wasn't going to add anything because there was nothing to add—yet. 'What about you? You never told me much, either.'

'It didn't seem relevant,' he agreed. 'I think you could probably sum it up in two words— work and pleasure. Neither of them was ever really satisfying. I spent far too many hours at my desk or flying around the world talking until I was hoarse. When I wasn't working I was trying to relax and I often used to think that was worse. When you can buy anything you want, you cease to want anything.'

Marisa frowned. 'By that you mean women?'

He threw her a sharp, piercing look. 'More or less.'

'More rather than less,' Marisa said with a sting.

Gabriel laughed under his breath. 'You don't seem to approve.'

'If it's what turns you on,' she shrugged, and saw his look of surprised amusement.

'It's not. It wasn't so much a question of getting turned on as of getting turned off. When I'd been working at full stretch for a while I needed to unwind, forget business.'

'So you found yourself a woman.' She could remember only too clearly the excited discussions which had gone on in the office whenever Gabriel publicly acquired a new lady companion. Their names had been common property. She had always known about his past life. What he was saying didn't surprise her. She had never felt she had the right to be jealous. You only have rights like that when you are emotionally involved, and Marisa had always struggled not to be emotionally involved with Gabriel.

'They never meant a damned thing,' said Gabriel, watching her face. 'I can barely remember most of them. There was always something missing. However lovely they were, I never missed them when they weren't there. They walked out of a room and out of my head at the same time. Now that's one thing I couldn't say about you. From the minute I saw you, you were right there in the middle of my mind and I couldn't shift you.'

'Did you try?' She had wondered what it was that made him so fiercely determined to marry her. After his wife died he had shown no sign of intending to marry again, despite obvious encouragement from the beautiful women who flicked in and out of his life.

'At first,' he said drily. 'I didn't just cave in and say to myself: she's my Waterloo. I told myself I was insane. Do you think you were the only one who recognised how crazy it was for us to get married?'

'It was,' she said, half smiling. It had been an act of monumental folly.

'Love is crazy,' said Gabriel, a gleaming amusement in his eyes. 'It hits you before you know what's going on and by the time you've realised it, you're already past doing anything about it. There should be a law against it.'

Marisa laughed. 'Perhaps you should speak to your M.P.'

'He wouldn't know what I was talking about. He's bald, fat and nearly seventy.'

'Poor man,' smiled Marisa. 'Maybe it's his wife you should talk to.'

'Wives have a habit of approving of love,' Gabriel said. 'If it's the marrying kind, of course.' She looked at him to smile and found him dangerously close, the hard face a few inches away, the grain of his skin brought into focus, every sharp detail of his features laid bare for her. Her eyes moved restlessly over that face, assessing the outward strength of it. Whatever you might say about Gabriel, he was a man you could rely on when you needed to lean on someone. She had leaned on him while Jamie was missing and it had eased the terrible strain of those hours to have him there. She hadn't thought about that until now. She had taken it for granted without even thinking.

His smile died suddenly. The grey eyes took on an expression she remembered all too well. 'You get to me, Marisa, you really get to me,' he muttered. 'God knows why—I certainly don't. I've asked myself over and over again what it was about you that made me want to grab you by the hair and drag you off, whether you wanted to come or not, and I still don't know. It may be just that you're so fragile. I've always felt I'd leave a bruise on you if I touched you with one finger.'

'I don't remember you being careful not to,' she said with a bitter little smile, remembering the night he had slapped her.

His skin grew hot, the grey eyes angry. 'Don't think I was proud of the way I behaved. I loathed myself. It was just that every time you turned away from me, something went snap inside my head. If just once you'd let me hope you might actually care for me . . .'

'You can't make people love you,' Marisa flung back. He had tried. He had been ready to force her to do whatever he wanted. That was one of the reasons she had always felt that he viewed her as a possession, a thing, without a will of its own.

'You never even tried,' he grated.

The emotional temperature between them had altered dramatically, the light calm way they had talked destroyed with an abruptness which took her by surprise. Which of them had ruined their brief truce? Whichever it was, the room was suddenly full of brooding tension, and she reacted to it as she had always reacted to any emotional threat, by starting to get up to run.

'No,' Gabriel muttered, his hand shooting out to pull her back towards him. The lines of his jaw had grown taut and his grey eyes were filled with angry emotion.

She thrust at him with both hands, struggling against the powerful grip, but she was too slightly built to be able to escape the pressure dragging her against him.

His mouth came down hungrily, one of his hands at her back, forcing her towards him, and in her fight to get free she tumbled forward, off balance, and found herself lying across him on the sofa. Gabriel put up one hand to take hold of her head and hold it. His mouth moved fiercely, compellingly, and Marisa's head began to swim as a heated wave of excitement clouded her brain.

The savage onslaught of his mouth softened as he felt her giving way. The kiss moved coaxingly, his hand tangled in her hair now, his fingers moving through the long strands and caressing her nape. She began to breathe rapidly, aware of the powerful body lying under her, the warm pressure of his thigh against her own. Her skin felt so hot she thought she was feverish, and her bones seemed to be melting inside her overheated flesh.

Fighting with that wild excitement was the old fear, the dread of loss, the flight from emotion. She wanted to give in entirely to this unbelievable passion, but she was too frightened.

She fought again to get free, pushing at his wide shoulders, and Gabriel said thickly, 'Let yourself go, darling. Stop fighting me.'

'I can't,' Marisa moaned, shuddering. She was torn between the fascination of the abyss and the fear of it, half of her longing to let go and fall in a headlong, abandoned flight and the other half pulling away from the edge as it sensed the total surrender which must follow.

'Oh, God!' Gabriel muttered savagely. 'Two years, two bloody years, I've been waiting to hold you again and you're still keeping me at arms' length. What do you think I'm made of?' His face pressed into her neck, his lips shaking as he moved them down her skin, the warmth of his breath coming faster, his body shivering with aroused desire as he held her down against him.

'Don't,' she whispered, her own lips trembling. Her fear was intensified by the hunger she could feel in him. It was bad enough to have to fight her own mounting need without knowing that Gabriel was out of control, his long hands caressing her with ruthless insistence, making her body burn wherever he touched it, his thigh moving with restless impatience against her.

'I need time,' she said, becoming angry. 'Gabriel, can't you understand anything? Stop rushing me. Give me time to think.'

'Oh, hell,' he groaned, wrenching himself away from her, their limbs disentangling with a violent movement which left her sprawling back on the sofa while Gabriel pushed to his feet and moved away, one hand running over his hair, his body still shuddering in that fierce excitement.

Marisa lay there, breathing unevenly, watching the back of his dark head in a nervous fixity. 'I'm sorry.'

'You're sorry? It seems to me that you don't know what you want,' Gabriel said hoarsely. 'You're not a child. You know how I feel.'

'I know how you seem to feel,' she argued.

'I want you desperately,' he said, still standing there with his back to her, his body taut.

'Want? Want? You talk like a little boy pointing to something in a shop window and bellowing for it. That's how Jamie carries on when we go past a sweet shop. He's not two yet, but you're an adult, for God's sake. You must realise you can't just say "I want" and expect to have it handed to you on a plate!' Her voice had become exasperated, slightly softened as she compared him to Jamie. She had so often thought how like his father Jamie was when he jumped up and down in his pushchair gabbling out a demand for sweeties.

Gabriel heard the alteration in her voice. He slowly turned on his heel and looked at her, the dark flush subsiding from his face, the tension going out of his body.

'So it seems,' he murmured wryly.

'Try to look at it from my point of view. We're only just beginning to know each other. Last time you rushed me into marriage and into bed before I was ready and it nearly blew my mind.'

He nodded, his mouth twisting. 'Very well, I'll wait. But don't take too long about it. My patience isn't inexhaustible.'

'You can say that again!' she muttered.

Gabriel laughed in a reluctant way, eyeing her with a curious gleam in his grey eyes. 'You know, you have changed. At first I thought you were exactly the same as you always were, but maybe that was owing to the terrible strain of worrying about Jamie. Now that you've started to talk I can see there's been changes during the past two years. Your mind is more confident, isn't it?'

'I don't know about my mind,' said Marisa, relaxing. 'I suppose I'm more confident, though. I've had to be. It wasn't easy bringing up a baby on my own. I've had to think for myself, for Jamie. Being responsible for him may have made me more responsible for myself.'

'Maybe that's it,' he agreed. 'You're more mature. You were very young for your age, and that wasn't saying much. At nineteen you were more like a fifteen-year-old, now you're more or less a woman.'

Her fine brows curved. She laughed. 'I'm not sure I like the way you phrased that!'

He gave her a mocking little smile, his black head tilted back and his long black lashes drooping against his cheek. 'You won't be a woman until you've come to terms with your own feelings, and you won't ever do that if you keep running away from them.'

Marisa slid off the sofa, her face averted. 'I'm not running away from anything.'

'No?' His voice murmured drily.

'No,' she said, walking to the door. 'I'm just . . .'

'Just what, Marisa?'

'Thinking about it,' she said, going out.

CHAPTER EIGHT

GABRIEL was right about one thing. Marisa's state of traumatic shock while Jamie was missing had concealed from him the changes which had taken place in her. Discovering that Jamie had vanished had wiped away the gains she had made during the past two years. All her hard-won confidence and belief in herself had been erased in a few minutes, and she had reverted to the disturbed, uneasy state of a woman in the grip of a deep fear. Shock can bring about regression, especially if the personality has always been uncertain, the belief in oneself never quite stable. Marisa had been dragged back into the past in a blinding flash and, since Gabriel had not seen her during the last two years, he had not realised until now the alterations which had been taking place in her in that time. He had seen the pale, silent girl he had known during their marriage, and imagined that she was just as she had always been.

If he had met her again the day before Jamie vanished, he would have seen a very different girl. Marisa had never been an exuberant, outgoing creature, but Jamie's love and dependence on her had given her an injection of confidence which she had lacked. She had learnt to laugh, to relax, to look outwards at the world and be prepared to meet it openly.

Jamie had been her passport to life. She had only had to produce him to have people smile at her, talk to her easily, the conversational path smoothed by his broad grins and curly head. At first she had found it hard. It had been an uphill struggle to talk to strangers, smile back cheerfully, make light chit-chat, but she had learnt how to do it gradually.

She had been so busy, so involved, always rushing from the house to work and back again, her days always filled to the brim and her mind always lively and active.

Now that she had Jamie back again she was relaxing back into her hard-won maturity. She realised she might have tremors of fear and uncertainty now and again whenever she remembered what had happened, but so long as she could look up and see Jamie there she would be able to feel safe.

All the same, she wasn't ready yet to make any decisions about her marriage. How could she let Gabriel rush her into a physical relationship when she didn't know how well she could cope with an emotional one?

She wanted to take it slowly, step by step, not tear headlong into an exchange of passion which might merely be a repetition of what had gone before. She might lose all her confidence, become an emotional cripple once more. She wouldn't let Gabriel do that to her.

This time she was the one making the decisions, forcing the pace. Gabriel was going to have to learn to be patient.

As Christmas advanced upon them, she was kept very busy making festive arrangements on a scale she had never had to face before. Last year she had only had to buy a tiny tree, a few presents, the bare minimum of Christmas food, but this year Mrs Dudley was determined to involve her in all the arrangements which someone in Gabriel's position would expect to have made. Most of them had been made long ago, of course. Gabriel's personal secretary had sent out his vast sack of printed Christmas cards and the smaller pile of personal cards to friends. She had also bought his Christmas gifts except those to really close friends, whom Gabriel had dealt with himself.

Mrs Dudley had made most of her own arrangements, too, but she insisted on consulting Marisa about them, all the same, urging her to suggest any changes she wanted made.

Gabriel had relatives across the country who descended on him at Christmas and who were expected this year, en masse, particularly since the publicity had made certain that they all knew that not only was Marisa back with him but that Gabriel now had a son and heir.

'I can cancel it all,' said Gabriel, his mouth wry. 'Shall I do that? Send them all telegrams, apologising?'

Marisa hesitated. Part of her longed to say yes. She didn't want to meet his relatives. She had met some of them before and she knew they had no higher opinion of her than Gabriel's friends had had. On the other hand, they were his nearest thing to a family and she did not feel she should interfere in arrangements that had been made months ago.

'No,' she said slowly. 'Let them come.'

He raised his brows, his face uncertain. 'Are you sure you can cope? I thought you found them stuffy, boring and condescending?'

'That's on their good days,' Marisa threw back tartly. 'On their bad days they drive me up the wall, but as the arrangements have all been made it's a bit late now to stop them. I've no wish to do so, anyway. I've no right to ask you to.'

'You've every right. You're my wife.'

'They're your family.'

His mouth twisted. 'A family I only see at rare intervals and with great reluctance. You're right about them—they're all the things you claim they are and a few more on top. I shan't cry if they never turn up again.'

'You must see something in them or you wouldn't have invited them all.'

'Invite them?' He laughed hollowly. 'They invite themselves. They tell me firmly that it's expected of me to give a Christmas do for the family. This house is big enough, God knows. They pack in here like sardines, but the house can take them. It's me who can't. Marisa, I'd much rather cancel it. Apart from the fact that I don't want to risk upsetting you all over again, I can happily go without seeing that lot of piranhas.'

She relaxed slightly, smiling. It made her feel better to know that Gabriel didn't care much more for his family than she did. 'No, let the arrangements stand. It's only for three days.'

'Three days can seem like eternity,' Gabriel groaned, running a hand through his thick black hair. 'Let's hope we survive it.'

Marisa looked at him, her blue eyes wide and thoughtful. There had been a note of genuine uneasiness under his voice. Did he, too, fear what his family would have to say when they arrived? Or, even worse, how they would look at her?

'What about Jamie's presents?' Gabriel asked, looking brighter. 'What shall we give him?'

'I've got him a sand lorry and a box of bricks,' Marisa told him.

Gabriel's glance was amused. 'That all? We can do better than that.'

'No,' she said succinctly, 'we can't.'

He caught the determined note in her voice, his eyes sharpening. 'We can't?' he repeated warily.

'Jamie doesn't need hundreds of toys. I won't have him spoilt. Two parcels will be quite enough for him. Any more than that and he'd soon get bored. His attention span isn't very great yet.'

'I stand corrected,' Gabriel drawled, his mouth twitching.

Her colour deepened. 'I'm sorry, I didn't mean to sound difficult, but . . .'

'But you've got strong views about what is or is not good for Jamie.'

'Yes,' she said, her mouth firming.

Gabriel looked at her with an amused smile. 'Can't I even buy him one tiny present of my own?' There was teasing in the grey eyes as they watched her.

She laughed. 'I'm sorry. Yes, of course, but nothing . . .'

'Too extravagant? No,' he promised, 'I won't go crazy. I don't want him spoilt, either.'

'It could be done so easily,' she said seriously, looking at him with a sort of pleading. 'And it wouldn't make him any happier to heap him with toys, it would only bore him.'

He touched her cheek with one finger, drawing the tip of it lightly down towards the corner of her mouth. She felt her skin tingling and her colour rising.

'When you're defending Jamie you can become quite belligerent, did you know that? Your blue eyes flash and you turn as stiff as a poker. Quite a frightening lady! I wouldn't like to take you on.'

Marisa moved away, smiling. She had been half dreading that little discussion. She had known it would come. If she and Jamie were staying, Gabriel was going to have to recognise that nothing was changing about the way Jamie was growing up. She had laid down a calm, loving routine for him from the moment she brought him home from the hospital. She had known what she wanted to give her son—all the things she had never had herself; love, security, warm protective care and a firm discipline. Children were like young plants. They needed to be

staked out with strong support, they needed
nourishment and warmth, a constant vigilance
which did not insist on digging them up to in-
spect their roots, a loving concern for their
growth and an enjoyment of them which was not
over-interfering.

The fact that Gabriel could give Jamie so much
more in a material sense than she would ever be
able to do alone, meant nothing compared with
the one thing she had always given, would always
give. Children could do without expensive
clothes, toys, all the trappings of a well-off
family. They couldn't do without love. It was, in
the last resort, the only thing that mattered, and
it made her and Jamie equal in an odd way, since
Jamie could give her back the love she gave him,
and, in giving it, confer on her just as much
happiness as she could give to him. Love made
them partners, linked them in a family circle, and
if Gabriel was to make one of that circle he must
accept the same rules as she and Jamie lived by.

Gabriel's family began to arrive on Christmas
Eve. Their cars rolled up to the front door and
disgorged their passengers one by one. Marisa
and Gabriel welcomed them together. She had
chosen to wear a warm woollen dress in a shade
of red which made her spirits lift. Colours
affected her. She felt happier as she looked at
herself in the dress. It made her feel that Christmas had really begun. Gabriel liked it, too.

'You look like a robin,' he mocked, his eyes on
the upward swell of her small breasts.

Her cheeks glowed. He was teasing her more and more often, his eyes filled with mocking invitation which never crossed over the invisible line they had drawn between them. Gabriel wasn't letting her forget that he was waiting for a sign from her, but he wasn't making the mistake of forcing the issue again.

Shaking hands with the next arrivals, Marisa realised that she was going to have a fight on her hands. It would be very polite, masked with sweet smiles and soft words, but it would be a fight, nevertheless. As she had expected, the Radley family were not exactly delighted to see her back with Gabriel. She hadn't been quite sure how they would handle it. Hostility, she had certainly suspected, but she hadn't been sure what form it would take. She was soon to find out.

'How old did you say the little boy was?'

Marisa turned her head to smile back at the elegant, silver-haired woman asking her that question, never guessing at that moment what lay behind it. 'Eighteen months.'

'Really?' Sylvia Crowley lifted her thin brows. She smiled, a bright cold movement of her thin mouth which made no pretence of warmth. Marisa saw the other guests looking at each other. Silent comment ran round the room.

Marisa's back stiffened as she finally caught on. Her eyes burnt with rage. They were hinting that Jamie was not Gabriel's child, she realised. Not a word was being said, of course; they were far too clever for that. They had always been far too clever for her. How could a shy, unsophisticated nineteen-year-old be any match for ultra-sophisticated women of their sort? While she blushed and stammered, they raised their brows, smiled, looked at each other in feline malice, making Marisa bitterly aware of her inadequacy. But she wasn't that tonguetied adolescent any more, she was a woman whose child was being used as a weapon against her, and the sly attack on Jamie sent a wave of blood to her head.

She did not make the mistake, though, of flaring openly. Instead, face coolly pleasant, she smiled back at Gabriel's cousin. She had always disliked Sylvia, she was a cat, but her claws weren't sinking into Marisa this time.

'It's so nice to have a real family party at Christmas, isn't it, darling?' Linking her arm through her husband's, she leaned on him, her slender shoulder brushing against his, and Gabriel gave her an amused, oblique smile.

'It's wonderful,' he said drily. He looked at Sylvia directly, the hard lines of his face forceful. 'You'll see my son later. Everyone keeps telling me how like me he is—I'm not sure I ought to be flattered. Every time I go near him he launches an attack on me. I think he has homicidal tendencies!'

Sylvia's face didn't move a muscle, but her eyes received the message Gabriel had just given her. The others got it, too. Gabriel was declaring himself firmly. Any further hints that Jamie wasn't his child should not be made in his hearing.

'I can't wait to see him,' Sylvia purred. 'At such a young age, of course, it's hard to tell who he really takes after.'

Gabriel's mouth became a straight line and he stared at his cousin with narrowed eyes. It surprised Marisa that Sylvia should continue to drop those spiteful hints, but then maybe Sylvia enjoyed causing trouble more than she valued Gabriel's favour.

'He certainly doesn't take after Marisa,' Gabriel said in a pleasant voice. 'Jamie's a little tough—a real Radley, I'm afraid, red in tooth and claw.'

There was some general laughter. Gabriel was cloaking it all with smiles, but they all knew it was war, and most of those present hurried to declare themselves on Gabriel's side. They might resent Marisa as much as Sylvia did, they might not understand why their powerful clan should have to put up with such a ridiculous marriage, but Gabriel was the most powerful member of that clan and his face warned them that this time they had to grin and bear it. Marisa was back to stay and Jamie was the new heir to the Radley millions.

'Such a terrible business, that kidnapping! It must have been so worrying for you.'

'We were horrified when we read about it in the papers. I would have rung to say how anxious and distressed we were, but we thought it was best not to ring, as you would have wanted to keep the lines free.'

'How anxious you must have been, my dear!'

They talked around Marisa, giving her commiserating smiles, cooing about Jamie, admiring her dress, saying what a difference it would make to have a child in the house at Christmas. She listened, scarcely distinguishing one from the other, smiling at them all, disliking them all so intensely that her teeth ached and her skin stretched painfully in those unreal smiles. They were all so alike, the women lacquered and beautifully dressed, the men smooth and presentable, their voices modulated and false, their smiles plastic. Several of them had brought their own children. They told her how nice it would be for their children to have a new cousin, what fun it would be for Jamie to have little friends.

'Oh, he'll think it's great fun,' Gabriel agreed, his eyes glinting. 'But you'd better make sure they wear armour. Jamie's great ambition in life is to take people apart and find out what makes them work. I think he's going to be a surgeon.'

Dudley circulated with a tray, proffering glasses of sherry with a smooth smile, his bald head tilted deferentially. He enjoyed these occasions; he had admitted as much to Marisa: 'I enjoy having the house full of visitors, madam.'

She had been tentatively hoping he would not be too hard pressed over Christmas with so much extra work, and he had reassured her. The house was looking even more elegant than usual. The women who came in every day to clean it had been working overtime. Dudley had seen to that, hovering around to make sure they brought the whole house to a pitch of perfection before Gabriel's family arrived.

As Dudley passed Marisa their eyes met. She distinctly saw one of his heavy lids droop in a wink. Startled, she looked at him again and Dudley's face was as bland as ever. Had she imagined it? He had already moved on and she couldn't be sure.

Gabriel slid his arm around her waist and drew her close to him. 'Rodney was wondering if we'd put Jamie's name down yet,' he said softly, giving her a grin.

'Name down?' She looked from him to one of the Radley men, her face puzzled.

'For the school,' Rodney explained earnestly. 'Get it down now, you know. Never too early. Want to make sure of a place.' He was a broad-shouldered man in his late forties, pink-skinned, blue-eyed, oddly fixed as he had been at around sixteen, the eternal schoolboy. 'We all do.'

Gabriel gave her a glimmering smile. 'Then we shall have to think about it, shan't we, darling?'

Marisa felt his long fingers just below the upward lift of her breasts, their pressure warm and confident. 'Yes, darling,' she said, smiling back, but her eyes wry, a little sardonic. Gabriel was teasing her and doing it because he knew that with all those politely hostile relatives of his around she was going to let him get away with it.

The possessive clasp of his arm, the exchanged smiles, were all intentional and all meant to underline for the Radley clan that Marisa was out of their reach, safe from the scratch of their claws. Gabriel had taken the message about the effect his family had had on her during the first year of their marriage. He was making quite sure that that sort of harassment didn't happen this time.

She would have preferred to have Christmas quietly with just herself, Jamie and Gabriel, but she began to think that perhaps it had been best to get this skirmish out of the way. Sooner or later the Radley family would have tried to undermine her again. They had been one of the factors which destroyed her marriage in the beginning; they were one of the factors which were making her hesitate about committing herself to Gabriel again. Until she felt she could take them on, deal with them without emotional damage to herself, she didn't feel she could think about her feelings for Gabriel himself. Marriage was more than just a relationship between a man and woman. She would have to become part of his family and if she couldn't cope with them her marriage wouldn't have a chance.

Dressing for dinner that evening she considered herself in the mirror, standing in front of the dressing table in bra and panties, her slender body pale in the soft glow of the lamp. She still looked absurdly young for Gabriel. But she felt much older now. Jamie had done that for her.

She wasn't just fighting for herself any more; she was fighting for Jamie's rights, Jamie's happiness, and she was prepared to take on the whole world if she had to.

The door opened. Gabriel tapped lightly as he walked in, but he had taken her by surprise. She stiffened, whirling to snatch up the white silk negligee from the bed in a defensive movement.

Gabriel closed the door, his eyes fixed on her as she hurriedly flung on the negligee and tied it round her small waist.

'My God, you're lovely,' he muttered, a flare of red coming into his face, moving towards her with a slightly unsteady haste.

'You should be getting ready,' she said huskily, very aware that he was only wearing a short white towelling robe, his long legs bare and damp under it from a shower.

He slid his arms round her waist, holding her against him, looking down into her wide, nervous eyes.

'I just wanted to say something,' he murmured, glancing down at the slender body so close to his own. 'But it went out of my head.' He bent his head and brushed the deep lace collar aside so that he could kiss her throat. 'I haven't seen you like this for so long. You're so tiny, Marisa. I don't know why that should turn me on so hard, but it does. It sends the blood to my head to see you in that thing.'

She put her hands on his arms to push him away, feeling a strange electric tingle as her fingers closed around his flesh. The robe had a faint dampness under her fingertips. 'We mustn't be late for dinner. We should be downstairs when the rest of them come down.'

'To hell with them,' Gabriel muttered hoarsely, moving his hot mouth along her neck.

'Gabriel,' she whispered, trembling.

'Yes,' he mocked, his mouth smiling unsteadily, and then he was kissing her possessively, one long hand stroking her hair, her face, her throat while the other moved in a convulsive exploration up and down her back. 'Marisa,' he muttered as he drew back slightly, 'tell me you want me. I'm going out of my mind. I don't think I can wait much longer. I'm only flesh and blood, and I can't stand it.'

She was burning, her whole body shivering with aroused excitement, her blue eyes looking back at him in helpless admission of her own response.

Giving a stifled half sob, half laugh, she protested: 'Not now, for heaven's sake, Gabriel!'

'Oh, God,' he said drily, closing his eyes. 'I wish I could turn the whole pack of them out of the house right this minute. I'm going to have to make polite conversation with the whole of my mind on one thing.'

Her lips trembled. 'You'll have to think of something else, then, won't you?'

'Witch,' he said, his grey eyes restless. 'I think you're enjoying this. You're deliberately holding me off, teasing me. Am I getting punishment,

Marisa? Is this your revenge for the way I rushed you into bed last time?'

She lowered her lashes, smiling a little. 'If you don't go and get dressed you're going to be late.'

'You are a tormenting little bitch,' groaned Gabriel, his hands dropping away. 'All right, I'm going.'

On this way to the door he stopped and looked round at her. 'Do you think you can learn to ignore my family? They aren't bothering you, are they? I thought you were coping with them very well earlier.'

'I don't exactly love them,' she admitted. 'But this time they aren't getting things all their own way.'

His grey eyes laughed. 'I did notice that. Sylvia's a vicious bitch. Take no notice of her.'

'If she makes any more digs about Jamie not being your son, I'll lose my temper,' said Marisa, her mouth settling into a hard line.

'It's amazing,' Gabriel commented.

'What is?' She looked at him sharply, ready to flare out at him if he gave her any excuse.

'What a difference Jamie has made to you. You look quite formidable when you get angry. You know, when you get older you're going to be quite striking. Your bone structure is so beautiful. I think that's what made me fall for you. I could see you were going to go on getting lovelier as you got older. Some women improve with age, others lose their looks. You're one of those who look more and more beautiful as they get old.'

Marisa laughed, giving him a sarcastic look. 'Go and get dressed, Gabriel.' She wasn't letting him flatter her so ridiculously. She knew she was not and never would be beautiful. She was far too thin, her high cheekbones and too wide mouth very far from beauty.

Gabriel gave her an answering smile. 'You don't believe me? I'm more perceptive than most men. I could see what you were going to be at one glance. Just remember, I told you first.'

He went out and, frowning, incredulous, she looked into the mirror at herself. Gabriel had to be crazy. Or blind. People said love made you blind, but this was absurd. He couldn't possibly think she was beautiful. She turned away from the mirror, her mouth twisting. No, Gabriel must have been flattering her without meaning a word of it.

CHAPTER NINE

WHEN Marisa got downstairs she found Gabriel
had arrived before her. He was in the drawing-
room, pouring himself a whisky, his head averted
from her as he concentrated on the decanter in
his hand. Marisa halted in the doorway, her eyes
flickering over the lean, formidable body, a peculiar heat in her throat. He was in evening dress,
the dark material enforcing the powerful impact
of his features, the black hair brushed flat and
tapering in to his nape in thick profusion.

As though suddenly sensing her presence he
half turned, his hand on the soda syphon, and his
eyes registered her with a narrowed intensity, his
breath drawn audibly.

His hand tightened on the syphon and soda
shot out, almost drenching his sleeve. He leapt
back, cursing, his face taking on a dark red
colour.

'Damn it!' He brushed his sleeve, his head
bent, and Marisa moved forward, rustling softly.

'Let me.' She took the handkerchief from him
and briskly dried his sleeve. Gabriel watched her,
his head just above her own, but she pretended
not to know that he was looking at her with that
absorbed awareness.

'You look fantastic,' he said huskily.

'Thank you.' She offered him the handkerchief. His fingers touched hers as he took it, a
tingling electricity running between them.

There was the sound of voices in the hall and
some of the others came in, talking and smiling.
They all stopped and stared at Marisa in open,
dazed disbelief.

'What can I get you to drink?' Gabriel asked
blandly, smiling. He was enjoying their expressions, although his own had been equally staggered.

Marisa had wound up her black hair on top of
her head and pinned it with a diamond star.
Every time she moved her head, the star glit-
tered, catching the eye. The hair-style had given
her long neck a swanlike beauty, her pale skin
softly unblemished, drawing the eye down to the
pleated bodice of her white silk dress. It was sim-
plicity itself, a fall of smooth material that clung
and rippled as she moved. The deep cleft of the
neckline gave tantalising glimpses of her white
breasts.

She looked as far removed from the skinny teen-
ager she had once been as careful attention to
detail could make her. The dress was a new one,
bought especially for the occasion. Gabriel hadn't
seen it before. Marisa had been determined to
surprise him as much as his family.

Sylvia came into the room and her catlike eyes
shot over Marisa in furious disbelief. Marisa gave
her a sweet smile.

'You look marvellous, Sylvia. What a lovely
dress!'

Sylvia showed her teeth in what could just pass for an answering smile. 'That necklace is quite superb, my dear. What a perfectly matched set of stones. Where did you find it, Gabriel?'

Bitch, Marisa thought, her eyes on her glass. Sylvia had been determined not to give her any compliment which could be suspected of being personal.

Gabriel shrugged calmly. 'I forget.' He laughed under his breath. 'It looks so good on Marisa it drives everything else out of my head.'

Marisa glanced up through her lashes. Gabriel was looking at his cousin, his hard face assertive, his eyes stony. Sylvia's colour rose and she moved away, fading into the other guests like someone trying to hide.

The rest of the evening passed without any sniping from Sylvia or any overt hostility from any member of the Radley clan. Looking down the long table at Gabriel during dinner, Marisa realised that they had got over the worst moments. With every word he said, every glance he gave her, Gabriel was signalling to his whole family that anyone who took her on was taking him on, too. Having recognised that, the Radley clan had regrouped and were ready to accept her with what grace they could muster. None of them could afford to offend Gabriel.

Over the Christmas period Marisa had overtures from a number of the guests. She realised that it was Jamie, again, who had made them switch attitudes. Jamie would be Gabriel's heir and, as Jamie's mother, Marisa was going to be very powerful. She did not make the mistake of imagining that any of the Radleys liked her any more than they had in the past. They were merely facing facts. The possession of Gabriel's son made her invulnerable to them.

She was ready to meet them halfway. She didn't want to go on battling with the Radleys if she could achieve some sort of polite truce. It didn't raise her opinion of them that they should suddenly become friendly because they recognised that if they offended her they would risk offending Gabriel, but she hid her feelings behind a smile.

On the evening of Boxing Day, they had a leisurely dinner and then danced for a few hours. The children had all been packed off to bed and the adults were torn between relief that the Christmas fever was over and a hectic determination to enjoy themselves before the return to work next day.

Marisa danced with a number of the men. They were pretty heavy weather. Those who weren't plain boring were inclined to pay her compliments which she suspected to be multipurpose ones, designed for any occasion and any female.

She rather liked Rodney best. He was hardly sparkling company either, but in his way he was sincere, mainly because he was too stupid to be otherwise, his earnest remarks delivered with that

schoolboy gaze, hovering between hopeful can-
dour and uncertainty.

While she was dancing with him for the second
time his brother tapped him on the shoulder.
'You've had your turn. Run away, Roddy, and let
me talk to Marisa.'

Rodney obeyed without hesitation, heading
straight for the decanters. Marisa looked up at
Martin Radley, her fine brows level. She did not
like him at all. He was around Gabriel's age; slim,
fashionably dressed, rather too pleased with himself, and convinced of his own charm and looks.

'Quite the dark horse, aren't you?' he asked her
as they danced, giving her a flattering smile.

'Am I?' She played it cool, letting him make
whatever point he was dying to make, not sure
yet whether he was intending to ingratiate himself with her or insult her.

'They all underestimated you. Thought they'd
seen the back of you when you ran off like that.
But you're smarter than the average bear, aren't
you?'

No, she thought, she did not like Martin
Radley. If he had been insulting her she might
have laughed but he thought he was flattering
her. That was much worse.

'Thank you,' she said limpidly, lowering her
eyes. There was no point in trying to answer him.

He was watching her when she looked up
again. His eyes wandered over her pale shoulders
in the ice-blue dress she was wearing, openly
admiring her in a way that made her teeth come

together. She had never enjoyed having men look at her like that. It was always a certain sort of man, one whose self-conceit made him impervious to everything but the satisfaction of his own ego. Martin Radley believed himself to be God's gift to the female sex. It didn't enter his head that his sexual appraisal might not be welcome to her.

'Gabriel's smart, too,' he added. 'I should have realised that he was too clever to make a mistake. You've really come on, you know. You're quite something when you're dressed up.'

'You're too kind,' Marisa said coldly, longing to hit him with something.

'Trust Gabriel to pick out a winner! His luck never fails.'

'I'll tell him you said so,' she smiled at him, and he laughed, looking amused.

'I shouldn't. Gabriel is touchy about his possessions.'

Marisa stiffened. 'I'm not one of them,' she retorted, her colour rising angrily.

Martin's eyes narrowed. She caught the bright gleam of them and wished she could recall the words. He moved nearer to her, smiling with all of the charm he could bring to bear, unaware, it seemed, that that phoney charm merely made her want to scream.

'You're your own property, are you? That's interesting. I admire a girl who has her head screwed on, especially one who can take on the family and beat them hands down. We have a lot in common, you know. I believe in independence, myself. Why don't we have lunch and talk about it?'

'Talk about what?' she asked, staring at him. Did he honestly think she was the sort of girl who would think like that?

He did. His smile held secret assurance, a conspiratorial enjoyment. 'Life, the family, whatever you have on your mind. What you need is an ally. They can be a very nasty bunch when they've got their minds set on it.'

'And they have their minds set on being nasty to me?' she enquired without really needing any answer.

'You're a threat,' he said cheerfully. 'Sylvia, now, she had her heart set on getting Gabriel married off to one of her daughters. She doesn't love you, our Sylvia.'

'I'm sorry to hear that,' said Marisa in a sweet voice. So that explained Sylvia's open resentment! Did Gabriel know about Sylvia's plans for him? Which daughter? Marisa wondered. Sylvia had three, none of them married. She looked around the room, her gaze in search of Gabriel, and found him dancing not far away. He was watching her in his turn. Their eyes collided and there was penetrating assessment in his grey stare. His eyes flicked from her to Martin, his features unrevealing. What was going on behind Gabriel's blank gaze? she wondered. He couldn't imagine she was enjoying Martin's over-obvious manner?

The music ended and someone shot over to put on a new tape. Martin looked at her with a lifted eyebrow. 'How about it, then? Lunch? I'll give you a ring next week, shall I?'

She had already had several social invitations from members of the family. They were falling over themselves to make it look as though they were delighted she was back. Martin's suggestion was in a totally different category, though. She knew what was behind his invitation.

'I'll have to discuss it with Gabriel, but by all means do ring us and we'll enjoy having lunch with you,' she said smoothly.

Martin's smile didn't flicker. His eyes altered slightly, that was all. Marisa smiled again and moved away. Gabriel joined her, a hand at her waist.

'And what was all that about?'

She looked at him, her face cool. 'Martin thought we might like to have lunch some time.'

Dudley was hovering about in the doorway. Marisa caught his eye and went over to him. 'I wondered what time to serve sandwiches and coffee, madam,' he asked quietly.

'You think they'll be hungry again this evening?' The kitchen had been kept permanently occupied in providing food, it seemed to her. The family appetite astonished her. Every few hours they all expected fresh supplies to come wafting up to them.

'In an hour or so, perhaps?' Dudley asked blandly.

'If you think they can cram more food in, Dudley,' she said. 'How's Mrs Dudley bearing up under the strain?'

He permitted himself a smile. 'She is quite enjoying it, madam. A challenge, you might say.'

As he vanished again Gabriel touched her elbow. 'Isn't it time we had a dance? I've had to watch you being the polite hostess to the rest of them. Now it's my turn.'

'I can play the polite hostess to you any time,' she said, looking at him through her lashes, smiling.

'If you can flirt with Martin, you can flirt with me,' he said, surprising her.

'I don't recall flirting with Martin!'

'No?'

'He may have been flirting with me,' she admitted.

'He was flirting with you,' Gabriel drawled. 'And for future reference, I didn't like it.'

She looked at him, her back stiffening. 'For future reference, you don't own me! I'm not one of your possessions, and if I do choose to flirt with anyone I will.' Turning away, she walked over to talk to some of the female Radleys, leaving Gabriel staring after her with a tight expression.

It had been absurd to get angry over his show of jealousy, but Martin had put her back up earlier when he referred to her as one of Gabriel's possessions. It had been that element in Gabriel's attitude to her that had really come between them in the past. Gabriel had so many possessions. He wasn't numbering her among them.

The party went on until three in the morning, although towards the end nobody was dancing and only the younger and more lively members of the family were determined to stay up and talk. Marisa couldn't go to bed until they had all gone upstairs. She stayed, fighting back yawns, so bored she was almost frantic, making polite conversation until her teeth ached.

When she did get to bed she fell asleep almost at once. When she woke up the bedroom was full of grey winter sunlight and her body was stiff from a sleep that had been too heavy.

She lay, yawning, stretching under the quilt. Her eye fell on the clock. 'Oh, God,' she moaned, flying out of the bed, 'Jamie!' Had anybody gone to him or was he screaming blue murder in his cot, waiting in vain for his breakfast? Dragging on a negligee, she ran to his room. It was empty. She sighed with extreme relief. Perhaps Mrs Dudley had gone in and taken him to the kitchen. Marisa hurriedly washed her face and dragged a comb through her hair before going downstairs.

The rest of the house was silent. The grandfather clock chimed eleven as she walked past it. Was everyone still asleep? She knew that some members of the family had planned to leave at dawn since they had long drives ahead of them, but there was no sign of anyone in the dining-room. Marisa went down to the kitchen and stopped in the doorway. Gabriel and Jamie were sitting at the kitchen table. In front of them was the box of bricks which Jamie had had for Christmas and they were absorbed in building a narrow tower. As Marisa watched Jamie placed one brick, his plump fingers unsteady. The whole tower wobbled and then crashed. Jamie looked startled for a second, his eyes nervous, then he threw himself back in his chair, laughing noisily.

'More,' he demanded.

'That's the sixth time,' Gabriel protested. 'Aren't you fed up with it yet?'

'More,' Jamie said, his chin thrust out obstinately. He slapped his small hand on the table. 'More, more!'

'You're a Radley, all right,' Gabriel observed with apparent satisfaction.

'Poor boy,' said Marisa.

Gabriel turned, grinning. 'Oh, up, are you? We wondered if you meant to sleep all day.'

'Where is everyone? There isn't a soul stirring.'

'Most of them have gone,' Gabriel told her. 'The others are dead to the world, including poor Mrs Dudley.'

Marisa glanced at Jamie who was showing her his pearly white teeth in a welcoming smile. 'Has Jamie had his breakfast?'

'Large amounts of it,' Gabriel moaned. 'I fed him some of that mushy cereal he loves. I wouldn't mind watching him eat it if he didn't chuck most of it about with such abandon.'

Marisa bent to kiss Jamie's nose. 'Having fun, darling?'

'He is,' Gabriel complained. 'I wouldn't say I

was. He seems to have an inexhaustible energy.
I've rebuilt that tower over and over again, but
he never gets tired of watching me.'

'Well, I'll go and dress, then,' Marisa informed
him, moving away, 'since Jamie is being so well
looked after.'

Gabriel said: 'Hey, come back! I'm not building that damn tower again.'

'You're loving it,' she mocked, going out.

'Bitch!' he yelled after her as she closed the
door, and she went upstairs, laughing. Despite
Gabriel's complaint she had seen the absorbed
enjoyment in both their faces. Jamie wasn't the
only one having fun. It was the first time Gabriel
had ever had his son to himself. He could start to
discover Jamie without her around to distract her
son's attention. She had eighteen months start on
Gabriel. He had a long way to go before he could
catch up.

Had Gabriel washed and dressed Jamie? she
wondered. Jamie had been buttoned into his
warm green sweater and the casual cord trousers
he wore when he was playing. Gabriel had gone
to bed at the same time as herself. Wasn't he
tired? Or didn't he need as much sleep as other
people?

When she had showered and dressed she went
downstairs to find some more members of the
family on their way. Submitting to a cool kiss
from them all, Marisa stood beside Gabriel and
watched their car slide away towards the gates.

'Is that the lot?' she asked.

'Yes, thank God,' Gabriel groaned. 'Until next

year.' He gave her a wicked smile. 'How about Christmas abroad next year?'

She didn't answer, walking back into the house. Mrs Dudley was in the kitchen now with Jamie in his high chair sipping milk through a red straw. He blew noisy bubbles into the milk as Gabriel appeared.

'He has some very anti-social habits,' Gabriel remarked to her. 'Did you know he eats soap?'

'Only if you let him,' Marisa pointed out. 'Your job is to stop him doing it.'

'Oh,' Gabriel grinned. 'I'll remember that. I wasn't sure if I ought to interfere. I wouldn't want to stop him expressing his personality.'

'Not by eating soap,' Marisa said. She removed the milk. 'You don't really want that, do you?'

'I think he does,' said Gabriel as Jamie threw himself about in the high chair screaming with rage.

'If he's blowing bubbles in it he doesn't want it,' said Marisa, lifting Jamie out.

'Now what?' Gabriel asked, following her.

'He ought to have some fresh air. I thought I'd take him for a walk.'

'Hang on while I get my coat,' Gabriel ordered, striding away. He came back in his sheepskin coat and opened the door for her, looking down at her as she pushed Jamie out into the cold winter air. Something in his grey eyes made her colour rise.

'What makes me get the feeling I'm on probation?' Gabriel asked her.

'I don't know,' she returned. 'What does?'

'Who's going to make the decision?' he asked without giving her an answer. 'You—or Jamie?'

She was startled. 'What?'

'Because I tell you here and now that, my son or not, I didn't marry Jamie, I married you. And it's not going to be up to Jamie whether we stay married or not.'

She stared after him as he walked ahead to open the gates. So that was what was in his mind? He thought she was waiting to see if Jamie took to him? Was that why he was making such an effort to win Jamie over to him?

Catching him up, she gave him a cool look. 'You're making it all too simple. Jamie is part of it, but only part. Your family was part of it, too. But in the last resort it comes down to how I feel. I know that.'

Gabriel's hard face was ironic. 'Well, that's a relief.'

Marisa's face tingled with heat and she looked away. The mockery in those sharp eyes made her prickle from head to toe. Did he think he would have a walk-over if she let her feelings decide the issue?

The trouble was, she was no longer sure exactly what the issue was—she had thought she knew a week ago, but in the intervening period so much had changed. Time had begun to spin a healing tissue over the trauma of losing Jamie. Marisa's confidence had begun to return. Her struggle with Gabriel's family had been resolved and she felt sure now that she could face his friends with the same confidence and outface them, too. She hadn't been capable of handling marriage with Gabriel Radley three years ago, but although she couldn't pretend even now that she was going to find it either easy or comfortable, she felt she wasn't going to be pushed around by circumstance any more.

The remaining issue was one which only she could resolve. It came down to the blunt question: did she want Gabriel? Was marriage to him what she really wanted for herself? Watching him with Jamie she had realised that Gabriel could be warm, loving, protective, all the things she wanted in a man. When he was amused or at ease that powerful face could relax into tremendous warmth, but at the back of her mind she still felt a peculiar unease.

She didn't know what gave birth to it—and until she did know she wasn't committing herself to him.

That evening after dinner they sat and talked, listening with half their minds to some music, pleasantly relaxed now that the house was empty again and all the Radleys gone back to wherever they had come from.

'It was really quite a success,' Gabriel observed.

'Would you say so?' Marisa couldn't be so certain.

'They came, they saw, they were conquered,' he mocked.

She lifted her eyebrows. 'I wouldn't put it like that.'

'I was scared stiff they might set off another explosion,' Gabriel said wryly. 'I'd rather have put off having them around until I was sure of you.'

The words made her hackles rise again. 'What makes you think you will be? Don't be so damned sure of yourself!' She got up and walked angrily to the door before Gabriel had time to catch her up.

In her room she began to undress, her face still flushed with anger. That was what it was, she thought. That was the stumbling block. Gabriel's possessive nature, his arrogance, his certainty that he would always get what he wanted—that was what was blocking her feelings for him. Last time he had just taken her, despite her confused and scared resistance, but he wasn't doing that again. She had established a belief in herself which she hadn't had in the past. If she let Gabriel resume possession of her the way he had before, she would be abandoning the hard-won position that Jamie's love and trust had helped her to achieve.

Gabriel opened the door and she turned on him, her face hectic with anger. 'Knock before you come into my room!'

'What the hell did I say?' Gabriel asked, coming in and shutting the door.

'Get out of here when I'm getting undressed!'

'What's the matter with you?' Gabriel was getting annoyed now, his face darkening with angry colour. 'What did I say that was so wrong? I've been patience itself for days. How much longer are you going to keep me kicking my heels outside your bedroom door?'

'For ever, if that's the way I want it,' Marisa flung at him, her eyes bitter. 'Get it through that thick head of yours—I belong to myself, not to you, and you're not adding me to your list of possessions, now or ever!'

Gabriel moved across the space between them, his teeth tight. 'Don't talk to me like that! I've never thought of you as a possession.'

'Oh, yes,' she said, thrusting away his hands as he tried to take hold of her shoulders, 'that's exactly how you thought of me. Well, not any more, Mr Radley. I belong to me.'

'I've told you,' he bit out hoarsely, 'don't push me away. I can't stand it.'

'You can't stand it? Isn't that too bad! You'll just have to learn to grin and bear it.'

'That's where you're wrong,' retorted Gabriel, tangling one hand in her hair and pulling her head back to expose her face.

'Don't you dare!' she muttered, struggling to get away.

His facial muscles clenched in on themselves, the bones in the hard face locked tight with rage. 'Hell,' he said, staring at her, 'one of us is crazy, and it isn't me. I know you want me.'

She drew a furious breath. 'You know nothing of the kind!'

'Oh, yes,' he threw back in a ragged tone. 'Yes, Marisa. I don't know what's keeping us apart, but I do know you want me. I knew that days ago.'

Her colour swept up in a hectic rush. Their eyes quarrelled and Marisa hastily looked away, biting her lip. There was a brief pause then Gabriel cupped her chin, his fingers gentle.

'I told you—you don't know what you want.'

'But you do, I suppose,' she said shakily, not meeting his gaze.

His voice was mocking. 'Oh, I do, yes.' His hand fondled her slender shoulder, ran softly down over her breast, making her body burn as he touched it. 'We both want the same thing, but you're refusing to admit it.'

'I won't be another one of the Radley possessions,' she said, wishing she could ignore the caressing movements of his hand. He slid it round her waist and drew her close to him.

'Forget that my name is Radley. Forget my family. Forget Jamie. Forget the whole damned world.' He tilted her chin and looked into her shifting blue eyes. 'Look at me, darling. Now— be honest with yourself and with me. Leaving everything but ourselves out of it, can you deny you want me?'

She swallowed, her throat very dry. 'You're not being fair.'

He laughed softly. 'Love isn't a question of being fair. There's no justice in love. Just answer the question.'

Marisa slackened, her body weak and submissive. Leaning forward, she let her face rest on his wide shoulder, feeling the comforting strength of it under her cheek.

'Does that mean yes?' he asked unsteadily, running his hand down her back.

She mumbled into his shirt, her lips shaking, and he framed her face between his hands, holding it tilted back, the dark hair falling over his hands.

'You had the guts to leave me. You had the guts to tell me you refused to be a Radley possession. Have the guts to tell me honestly that you want me, Marisa.' His grey eyes were gleaming with excited amusement and mockery which was underlaid with a totally different feeling.

'Damn you!' Marisa sighed.

'Say it,' Gabriel ordered, watching her intently.

'I want you!' she almost shouted, then jumped as the sound ran round the room in a sort of echo.

Gabriel started to laugh in a husky, delighted amusement. 'At last!' he grinned, lifting her up into his arms and moving with her towards the bed.

'That doesn't mean . . .' she began as he laid her on the bed and joined her, his breath beginning to come fast and thick.

'Tell me later,' said Gabriel, his black head swooping. Against her yielding mouth he whispered, 'Much later.'

Take these
4 best-selling novels FREE

That's right! FOUR first-rate Harlequin romance novels by four world renowned authors, FREE, as your introduction to the Harlequin Presents Subscription Plan. Be swept along by these FOUR exciting, poignant and sophisticated novels . . . Travel to the Mediterranean island of Cyprus in **Anne Hampson**'s "Gates of Steel" . . . to Portugal for **Anne Mather**'s "Sweet Revenge" . . . to France and **Violet Winspear**'s "Devil in a Silver Room" . . . and the sprawling state of Texas for **Janet Dailey**'s "No Quarter Asked."

Harlequin Presents...

The very finest in romantic fiction

Join the millions of avid Harlequin readers all over the world who delight in the magic of a really exciting novel. SIX great NEW titles published EACH MONTH! Each month you will get to know exciting, interesting, true-to-life people . . . . You'll be swept to distant lands you've dreamed of visiting . . . . Intrigue, adventure, romance, and the destiny of many lives will thrill you through each Harlequin Presents novel.

Get all the latest books before they're sold out!

As a Harlequin subscriber you actually receive your personal copies of the latest Presents novels immediately after they come off the press, so you're sure of getting all 6 each month.

Cancel your subscription whenever you wish!

You don't have to buy any minimum number of books. Whenever you decide to stop your subscription just let us know and we'll cancel all further shipments.